Where lost dogs heal lonely hearts…

Marion Lennox brings you four wonderfully warm, witty, emotional and uplifting stories with happy endings you'll never forget.

Step into Banskia Bay, a picturesque seaside town where hearts are made whole and dreams really can come true! With the help of a few mischievous little dogs, couples get together and find that they are in for journeys they had never expected….

Available now:

Abby and the Bachelor Cop
Misty and the Single Dad
Nikki and the Lone Wolf
Mardie and the City Surgeon

Dear Reader,

Last month, appalling floods swept over much of inland Australia. My brother still runs my family's dairy farm. He knew water was sweeping down from the north, and in preparation he drove his cows to higher country. Not high enough. At midnight, he went to check and found seventy calves fighting for their lives. In the middle of the paddock was a patch of high ground where four could find a foothold. The rest were swimming.

The water was too deep for him to reach them. None of them were leaving the perceived safety of that tiny patch of higher ground. So back home he went to fetch the kids' battered kayak. Then back to the flood. Beside him was his ancient border collie. She's blind, but in the dark, blind was almost an advantage.

One man in a kids' kayak. One border collie determined not to be left behind. My sister-in-law on gate and general holler-and-worry duty. They saved them all. Heroes, all three.

And thus I decided that one blind border collie needed her own story. Bessie, my fictional dog, is a mixture of all the dogs who've ever worked their hearts out for my family. Mardie and Blake, my hero and heroine need to be truly heroic to deserve her, and to deserve their own happy ending. I hope they make the grade. You decide.

Marion

MARION LENNOX

Mardie and the City Surgeon

BANKSIA
BAY

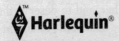

TORONTO NEW YORK LONDON
AMSTERDAM PARIS SYDNEY HAMBURG
STOCKHOLM ATHENS TOKYO MILAN MADRID
PRAGUE WARSAW BUDAPEST AUCKLAND

Recycling programs
for this product may
not exist in your area.

ISBN-13: 978-0-373-17784-4

MARDIE AND THE CITY SURGEON

First North American Publication 2012

Marion Lennox is a country girl, born on an Australian dairy farm. She moved on—mostly because the cows just weren't interested in her stories! Married to a "very special doctor," Marion writes for the Harlequin® Medical™ Romance and Harlequin® Romance lines. (She used a different name for each category for a while—readers looking for her past romance titles should search for author Trisha David, as well). She's now had more than seventy-five romance novels accepted for publication.

In her non-writing life, Marion cares for kids, cats, dogs, chooks and goldfish. She travels, she fights her rampant garden (she's losing) and her house dust (she's lost). Having spun in circles for the first part of her life, she's now stepped back from her "other" career, which was teaching statistics at her local university. Finally she's reprioritized her life, figured what's important and discovered the joys of deep baths, romance and chocolate.

Preferably all at the same time!

Books by Marion Lennox

CHRISTMAS WITH HER BOSS
MISTY AND THE SINGLE DAD*
ABBY AND THE BACHELOR COP*
NIKKI AND THE LONE WOLF*

*Banksia Bay

Other titles by this author available in ebook format

To John and Joy, for giving life to my books,
as well as saving calves at midnight.

CHAPTER ONE

IT WAS a dark and stormy night. Lightning flashed. An eerie howl echoed mournfully through the big old house.

The lights went out.

She *had* to stop watching Gothic horror movies, Mardie Rainey decided, as she told Bounce to cut it out with the howling and groped to the sideboard for candles. She especially had to stop watching horror movies on nights when a storm was threatening to crash through her roof.

Bounce, her twelve-month-old border collie, was terrified. Mardie was more irritated than spooked. The vampire had been sinking his fangs when the power went off. Now she'd never learn what happened to the fluff-for-brains heroine who would have been a lot more interesting with fang marks.

What a night. The wind was hitting the chimney with such force it was cutting off the draw, causing smoke to belch into the room. She was down to a few candles and a flashlight.

There was a leak in the corner of the room. She'd put a bucket underneath. Without the sound of the television, the steady plinking was likely to drive her crazy.

She should go to bed.

A crash, outside. A big one.

Bounce stared at the darkened window and whimpered. The hairs on the back of his neck stood up.

'It'll be one of the gums in the driveway,' she told him,

feeling sad. She loved those trees. 'That's for tomorrow and the chainsaw.'

There wasn't a lot she could do about it now.

Bounce was still whimpering.

She took his collar and headed for the bedroom. 'It's nothing to worry about,' she told him. 'We don't have trees close enough to hurt the house. Lightning and thunder are all flashy show, and I warned you about watching vampires.'

Bounce whimpered again and pressed closer. So much for guard dogs.

Normally he slept in the kitchen. Not tonight.

It really was a scary night.

Maybe she did need vampire protection, she conceded as she headed for bed. Bounce might be a wuss but the only alternative was garlic. A girl couldn't sleep with garlic.

'Bed's safe,' she told him. 'The sheep are in the bottom paddock and that's protected. The house is solid. Everything's fine. At least we're not out in the weather. I pity anyone who is.'

Blake Maddock, specialist eye surgeon, should have stayed the night in Banksia Bay, but he wanted to be back in Sydney. Or better still, he wanted to be back in Africa.

He'd wanted to leave Banksia Bay the minute he'd discovered Mardie wasn't there.

What sort of stupid impulse had led him to attend his high school reunion? Wanting to see Mardie? That had been a dumb, sentimental impulse, nothing more. As for the rest, he'd turned his back on this place fifteen years ago. Why come back now?

Nothing had changed.

Or…it had a little, he conceded as he drove cautiously through the rain-filled night. But not much. There'd been births, deaths and marriages, but the town was just as small. People talked fishing and farming. People asked where he was living now, but weren't really interested in his answer. People asked did he miss Banksia Bay.

Not so much. He'd left fifteen years ago and never looked back.

Three miles out of town was his old home—his great-aunt's house. He'd been sent here when he was seven, to forget Robbie.

Ten years ago, sorting his great-aunt's estate, he'd found a letter his father had written to her after Robbie's death.

We don't know where else to turn. His mother never warmed to the twins, to boys. Now... They were identical, and every time she looks at him she feels ill. She's drinking too much. Her friends are shunning her. We need to get the boy away. If we can tell people he's gone to relatives in Australia so he won't be continually reminded of his brother, the pressure will ease. Can we send him to you, for however long it takes until his mother wants to see him again?

And underneath was the offer of a transfer of a truly astonishing parcel of shares of the family company.

How much had his parents wanted to get rid of him?

He knew now, how much.

So a bereft seven-year-old had been sent to the other side of the world, to a reclusive great-aunt who'd run away herself, years before, after a failed romance. Who'd been kind according to her definition of the word, but who'd lived in the shadow of her own tragic love affair and never spoke about Robbie.

No one spoke about Robbie. No one here knew.

'Don't tell people about your brother,' his father had told him as he saw him onto a plane. 'Least said, soonest mended. I know it wasn't all your fault—your brother was equally responsible. Your mother will accept that in time. Meanwhile, get on with your life.'

His life as a kid no one wanted. His life in Banksia Bay.

It was dumb to have come tonight, he conceded. This had been his place to hide, to be hidden, and he had no need of that now.

And Mardie hadn't even attended.

Mardie had been in the year below him at school. His one true thing.

He remembered the first day he'd attended Banksia Bay School, dropped off by his silent great-aunt, feeling terrified. He remembered Mardie, marching up to him, littler than he was, all cheeky grin and freckles.

'What's your name? Did you bring lunch? I have sardine sandwiches and chocolate cake; do you want to share?'

How corny was it that he remembered exactly what she'd said, all those years ago?

It was corny and it was dumb. It was also dumb to think he might see her tonight. He hadn't thought it through.

He wasn't actually in a frame of mind where he could think anything through. He'd flown in from Africa exhausted. Dengue fever had left him flat and lethargic. It was four more weeks at least before he could return to work, he'd been told.

What work?

Bleak thoughts were all over the place. He'd stayed at his great-aunt's apartment in Sydney, the place she'd kept for shopping. He'd kept it because it was convenient, somewhere to store his scant belongings. It was the only place he could vaguely call home. Listlessly he'd checked mail that hadn't been redirected since he'd been ill, and found the invitation to the Banksia Bay reunion.

And he'd thought of Mardie. Again.

For some unknown reason, during this last illness Mardie had strayed into his thoughts, over and over.

Why? She'd have forgotten him, surely, or he'd be a distant memory, a blur. Theirs had been a childhood friendship, turning into a teenage romance. She'd be well over it. But… he wouldn't mind seeing her.

Could he drive to Banksia Bay and back in a night?

The question hung, persisted, wouldn't listen to a sensible no.

He'd decided years ago that Banksia Bay, the place where his parents had abandoned him, the place where he'd been sent to forget, was a memory he needed to move on from. But now, with his career uncertain, his focus blurred by illness, the reasons for that decision seemed less clear.

And his memory of Mardie was suddenly right back in focus.

Two hours there, four hours for dinner, two hours back. Okay, he'd be tired, but he didn't want to stay in Banksia Bay. Doable.

So he'd put on his dinner suit, driven from Sydney, sat through interminable speeches, too much back-slapping and too many questions. All on the one theme. 'Isn't it wonderful that you're a doctor—have you ever thought about coming home?'

This wasn't home. It was the place he'd been dumped after Robbie.

And of course Mardie wasn't at the dinner. He hadn't realised it was a reunion for just the one class.

He'd left as soon as he could. He should have gone straight back to Sydney.

But the thought of Mardie was still there. He'd come all this way…

Could he casually drop in at ten at night?

Um…maybe not.

The trees on the roadside were groaning under the strain of gale-force winds. The windscreen was being slapped with horizontal sleet.

Mardie's farm was right here. If it was daylight he would be able to see it.

Why did he want to see her?

She'd been a kid when he left Banksia Bay. Sixteen to his seventeen. She was probably married with six kids by now.

The impossibility of dropping in was becoming more and more apparent. On a moonlit night, maybe. If he'd rung ahead, maybe. He knew her phone number—he'd had it in his head for twenty years. As he'd left the reunion he'd thought he'd see if her lights were on and then he'd ring, and if she answered, he'd take it from there.

Only of course he'd forgotten there was no cellphone reception out here. Or maybe he'd never known. He'd left practically before cellphones were invented.

Enough. He needed to get back to the highway, put sentiment aside and focus on sense.

Focus on the road.

A blind bend. Darkness. Rain.

Mardie's house was a couple of hundred yards from the road. No lights. So that was that. Maybe she'd moved.

Of course she'd moved. Did he expect her life to have stood still?

And then…a dog, right in the middle of the road.

He hit the brakes, hard.

If it wasn't wet he might have made it, but water was sheeting over the bitumen, giving his tyres no grip.

His car skidded, planing out of control. He fought desperately, trying to turn into the skid, trying…

A tree was in front of him and he had nowhere to go.

Bounce was quivering beside the bed, flinching at each clap of thunder. Growling at the weird shapes made by lightning.

'You're starting to spook me,' Mardie told him as she snuggled under the covers. 'One more growl and you're back in the kitchen.'

The next clap of thunder sounded almost overhead and suddenly Bounce was right under the duvet.

Farmer with working dog. Total professionals. Ha! She hugged him, taking as well as giving comfort.

'We're not scared,' she told Bounce in her very best Farmer-In-Charge-Of-The-Situation voice.

Thunder. Lightning. The house seemed to tremble.

Another crash.

This one had her sitting up.

Uh-oh.

For the last crash was different. Not thunder. Not a falling tree.

It was the sound of tyres screaming for purchase, and then impact. Metal splintering.

And then?

And then it looked as if she was braving the elements, like it or not.

He wasn't hurt. Or not much. There was a trickle of blood on his forehead—the windscreen had smashed and a sliver of metal or glass must have got past the airbags. But he'd hired a Mercedes. If there was one thing these babies were good at it was protecting the occupant.

One of his headlights, weirdly, was still working. He could see what had happened. The trunk of the tree had met the front of the car square on. The whole passenger compartment seemed to have moved backward. The windscreen seemed to have shifted sideways.

The tree was about a foot from his nose.

Rain was sheeting in from the gap where the windscreen had been.

He ought to get out. Fire…

That was a thought forceful enough to stir him from his shock. He was out of the car in seconds.

A dog met him as he emerged, knee height, wet, whining,

nuzzling against him as if desperate for reassurance from another living thing.

The dog. The cause of the crash.

He should kick it into the middle of next week, he thought. Instead, he found himself kneeling on the roadside, holding it, feeling shudders run through the dog's thin frame. Feeling matching shudders run through his.

They'd both come close to the edge.

He tugged the dog back a bit, worried the car might blow, but it wasn't happening, not in this rain. Any spark that might catch was drenched before it even thought about causing trouble.

The sparks weren't the only thing drenched. Thirty seconds out of the car and he was soaked.

What to do? He was kneeling beside his crashed car in the middle of nowhere, holding a dog.

He was four miles from Banksia Bay, and Banksia Bay was in the middle of nowhere. It was a tiny harbour town two hours from Sydney, set between mountains and sea. He'd already checked for phone reception. Zip.

He had a coat in the car. He had an umbrella.

It was too late for coats and umbrellas. He was never going to be wetter than he was right now.

The dog whined and leaned heavily against him. A border collie? Black and white, its long fur was matted and dripping. The dog was far too thin—he could feel ribs. It was leaning against him as if it needed his support.

He put a hand on its neck and found a plastic collar, but now wasn't the time to be thinking about identification.

'We're safe but we're risking drowning,' he said out loud, and he stared through the rain trying to see Mardie's house.

Dark.

Still, it was the closest house. It was over a mile back to his aunt's old home which, someone had told him tonight, had become a private spa retreat, but was now in the hands of the receivers. Deserted. After that… He couldn't think.

The trees around him were losing branches. He had to get out of the weather.

Did Mardie still live here?

How ironic, after coming all this way because he'd stupidly assumed she'd be at the school reunion, to end up on her doorstep like a drowned rat. Waking her from sleep.

Crazy.

His head hurt.

He had no choice.

He turned towards the house and the dog plodded beside him, just touching.

'Mardie and a husband and six kids?' he asked the dog. 'Or a stranger.' And then, despite the rain, despite the shock, he found himself grinning. 'I came all this way to find Mardie. It seems fate's decided I'm still looking.'

The phone was dead.

There was no mobile reception here ever, but she did have a landline. Not now. The lines must be down.

She was on her own.

A car crash.

This was worse than vampires. Much worse.

She hauled on her outdoor gear at lightning speed, her sou'wester with its great weatherproof hood, her waterproof over-pants and her gumboots. She grabbed her most powerful flashlight.

Bounce refused to come out from under the bedcovers.

'Watch the house, then,' she conceded, thinking she'd be better without him anyway. She'd like the comfort of his presence but if it was a disaster…

She'd need an ambulance, not a dog.

She felt more alone than she'd ever felt in her life.

'It's you or no one,' she said savagely to herself and hauled open the door.

To be met by Blake Maddock.

How could you not see someone for fifteen years and know in an instant that you were looking at the same man?

She did. She was.

At seventeen, Blake Maddock was the best-looking guy in grade school. He was tall, dark and drop-dead gorgeous. He had deep black hair and skin that seemed to tan without the sun. At seventeen he'd needed a bit of filling out, but not any more.

This was Blake Maddock all grown up.

The grown-up version of Blake Maddock was wearing a black dinner suit, black bow tie, white shirt and silver cufflinks.

His jet-black hair was dripping. His suit was sodden.

Blake.

She must be dreaming.

But it didn't pour with rain in dreams, or she didn't think it did. This wasn't an apparition. Blake Maddock was standing on her veranda.

'Mardie?' he said, and she figured he couldn't see her. She was in the hallway and of course it wasn't lit. The lightning was almost continuous now though, and whenever it forked it lit the veranda as bright as daylight. She could see him, over and over again.

Blake.

'H…hi,' she managed but she stuttered the word. She tried again but the stutter got worse.

'It is Mardie?' he said, trying to see.

'Y…yes.'

She caught herself and stepped outside. The wind practically knocked her sideways.

A black shadow moved from Blake's side to hers. It leaned against her legs as if seeking refuge.

Blake Maddock and dog. What the...?

Her mind stopped whirling. The night slid away. Blake Maddock was right in front of her—Blake, her very best of friends.

She grabbed his hands and held on, and he stared down at her and attempted a half smile. She stared up at him, incredulous. His smile twisted, self-mocking, and it was the smile she remembered. Blake...

His smile faded. He stared down at her in the weird light provided by lightning—and then he tugged her into a bear hug.

She let herself be tugged. He was soaked to the skin. He was bigger than she remembered, taller, *harder*.

She let herself be crushed against his chest. Right this minute, all she could feel was joy.

'Blake.'

It was barely a whisper. Her past had returned. Her past was dripping wet on her veranda.

Her past was hugging her as if he'd missed her as much as she'd missed him.

Another crash of thunder, deeper, longer. This was no night for standing in the sleet, hugging. He put her at arm's length, but still he held her, hands gripping hers. As if holding on to reality.

'I've crashed my car,' he said and she thought...she thought...

She didn't think anything. She was too flabbergasted.

'Where...? Why...?'

'I've come from the school reunion.'

The school reunion. Things settled. Just a little.

She'd heard what was happening—a reunion for the class above hers from fifteen years ago. Tony Hamm, the local butcher, had been organising it. Her friend Kirsty had told her about it when she was in the local store this morning.

'They're so excited. But dinner suits… That's only because Jenny Hamm wants to wear the dress she bought for her sister's wedding. You should hear the complaints.'

Tony's class.

Blake's class.

She'd thought then…

Yeah, she'd thought, but she hadn't said. She hadn't asked: *Is Blake Maddock coming?*

Obviously he was. Obviously he had.

He was on her veranda.

He'd said he'd crashed his car. There was a trickle of blood on his forehead. She struggled to get her confused mind to focus.

'There's blood…' she managed. 'Your head…'

'A scratch. I'm fine.'

'Really?'

'Really.'

She was getting her breath back. She hadn't seen this guy for fifteen years. There were so many emotions in her head she didn't know what to do with them.

'Get into the hall,' she managed. 'Out of the wind.' She pulled away, then stood aside and ushered him into the entrance porch. As if he was a casual acquaintance.

'Is anyone else hurt?' Her voice sounded funny, she thought. 'The other car…'

'Only me,' he said, and his voice astonished her. Deep and rich and growly. All grown up. 'I hit a tree.'

'A tree?'

'I'm not drunk,' he said, and he truly was Blake, his voice touched with the lazy humour she knew so well. 'I've been to the reunion dinner. They served Tony Hamm's home-made beer and Elsie Sarling's first attempt at making Chardonnay. It wasn't a struggle to stick with water.'

Her lips twitched in return, smiling back. Tension eased. An old school friend in trouble. She could do this. 'So the tree?' she said cautiously.

'It jumped out and hit me.' He sighed. 'No. The dog jumped out. I managed to miss the dog. I hit the tree instead.'

He'd hit a tree. A car crash, late at night. Blake.

So many emotions…

Priorities. 'Is the car blocking the road?' she managed and was absurdly proud of herself for sounding so sensible.

'No. I was aiming to miss the dog and I made a good fist of it. It's well off.'

That, at least, was a plus. She didn't need to get the tractor and drag a wreck from the road to stop others crashing into it.

She could focus on Blake.

Or actually…not. Focusing on Blake made her feel weird, like stepping through the wardrobe into Narnia, into another world. The world of fifteen years ago. Concentrate on the dog, she told herself. The dog seemed far less complicated.

It was a border collie, mostly black, with touches of white. It, too, was wet to the bone. She felt it shudder against her legs, and it was a far deeper shudder than Bounce's vampire-and-thunder-induced shudder.

If there was one thing that could touch Mardie Rainey's heart, it was a dog. A wet and obviously frightened dog was always going to hit her heart like an arrow. It even distracted her from Blake. She knelt down to see, to pat.

'Hey, sweetheart, where did you come from?'

But then she felt its collar, and she knew.

A ribbon of plastic.

She knew this collar.

'Oh, no.'

'Not yours?' Blake asked.

'No. This is a pound dog.' She fingered the collar, feeling ill. 'The local Animal Welfare van crashed last week and dogs escaped. Stray dogs are turning up everywhere. This collar says this is one of them.'

But this was a border collie.

Farmers round here valued their dogs above diamonds. Border collies were natural workers. For one to end up in the pound didn't make sense.

But she could only concentrate on the dog for so long. The dog was distracting, but not distracting enough.

She had Blake Maddock in her front porch.

'Mardie, I'm in trouble,' Blake said above her. The momentary emotion that had given rise to the hug had faded, leaving manners. 'Would your mother object if I came in to dry off and ring for help?'

Would her mother object?

Memories of the last time she'd seen Blake flooded back. Blake in this house, in this kitchen. Blake kissing her senseless.

'Come to Sydney,' he'd said urgently, holding her close. 'You're smart. You could get a scholarship. There's stuff we can do, Mardie. We can make a difference. Come with me. You can't be happy here.'

She remembered her whole body melting as Blake kissed her so deeply she thought she surely must say yes. She remembered his hands slipping under her blouse, and she remembered the hot, aching need.

But she was sixteen and her mother was suddenly there, confronting them with anger. Her mother was so seldom angry it jolted them both.

'Blake, it's time for you to go home. Mardie and I need to be up early, to draft the sheep ready for crutching.'

And, as she'd spoken, Mardie had seen fear.

Her mother had heard what Blake had said. She'd heard him asking her to go to Sydney.

She'd known, even then. At sixteen, the weight of this farm was on her shoulders.

You can't be happy here... Why not?

She loved Banksia Bay, and she loved farming. She'd also loved Blake, with every shred of her sixteen-year-old being.

But Blake couldn't wait to be off. He was heading to Sydney to do medicine.

She could get a scholarship? To do what? Something to make a difference? What was he talking about?

She loved her art, she loved making things, but even then she'd known Blake saw her passion as not to be taken seriously.

Even then she'd known they were moving in different directions.

'Write,' she'd told him, feeling desolate.

'Follow me to Sydney. Finish school and apply to the same university. I'll wait for you.'

She still remembered the desolation. 'I don't think I can. Blake, please write.'

'And just be friends?' he'd demanded, incredulous. Her mother was waiting stolidly for him to leave. She moved into the living room, out of hearing but not out of sight. 'We've gone too far to be just friends.'

She thought of that statement now. It had been an adolescent ultimatum: follow me to Sydney, move in my direction or cease being my friend.

All or nothing.

It had to be nothing.

She'd watched him go and her sixteen-year-old heart felt as if it was breaking.

And now he was back—grown, changed, but still Blake. He was watching her face, reading her warring emotions as he'd always been able to read her emotions. 'Is your mother...?' he started.

'Mum's fine,' Mardie said.

'She's asleep?'

'It's midnight.' She hadn't seen this man for half a lifetime. Use your head, she told herself. There was no way she should tell this…stranger…that she was home alone. Let him think her mother was still sleeping in the front room.

Even if he had hugged her.

Even if he was Blake.

'Did I wake you?' he asked. 'I'm sorry.'

'I was still awake. A tree came down and then I heard the car crash. I was coming to find out.'

'If you could turn on a light…' Blake ventured.

'No power. But come in anyway. Are you…are you really okay?'

'Shaken, not stirred.'

And at that…she smiled.

James Bond movies had been their very favourite thing. That last year together, a new movie had come out. She remembered persuading her mother to take them to Whale Cove. Dressing up. Standing hand in hand in the queue, waiting for tickets. She'd looked as glamorous as a sixteen-year-old on limited means could manage. A home-made dress, all slink and crazy glamour. Stilettos from the second-hand market. Blake had worn a dinner suit, probably not even hired. Money was never a problem for Blake. He'd looked a fairly adolescent Bond, but at sixteen she'd thought he'd looked a Bond to die for.

Shaken, not stirred.

Right now she was stirred.

She stood aside to usher him into the house. His body brushed hers as he passed.

There was no way she could feel him through her waterproofs.

She felt him. Every nerve in her body felt him.

This was weird. A teenage love affair, long over.

It was the night, she told herself. Her fear from the crash. The appalling storm. A boy she'd once loved.

A man, she told herself sharply. A stranger. She needed to be practical, sensible, and together.

'The dog…' he said.

'Dogs are welcome in this house.' Even stray and sodden ones. Maybe especially stray and sodden ones. 'Go through to the kitchen,' she said. 'It's warmer. I'll find towels and shed my coat.'

They were operating by flashlight. She lit a candle on the hall table and handed it to him.

The lightning outside was almost one continuous sheet. The house went from dark to light, from dark to light…

'This isn't James Bond,' he said. 'It's Gothic Horror.'

Gothic Horror… Her thoughts exactly. He'd always been on the same wavelength. The thought was…unsettling.

Unsettling but good. As if a part of her was suddenly restored.

There was a crazy thought.

'If you've grown fangs since I last saw you, I'm heading into the night right now,' she muttered. 'Kitchen. Go. Now.'

The dog whimpered and pressed closer against her.

'Leave her with me,' she said as he hesitated.

'She's my responsibility.'

'You brought her to me,' she said. 'One dog doesn't add very much to what I take care of.'

'Mardie…'

'Just go.'

After fifteen years, Blake Maddock had walked back into her life.

For some stupid reason, her head felt as if it was exploding.

Blake. A childhood friend. A teenage boyfriend. Nothing more.

Focus on the dog. Nothing else.

She headed for the linen closet and the dog stayed with

her, its body still just touching her leg. She crouched in the dim light and ran her hands over the sodden coat and the dog whined a little and pressed in closer.

A female. Full grown. Trembling without pause.

There was no obvious wound. She didn't seem tender to touch.

She needed to get her into the light. Into the kitchen, where she had a bigger store of candles.

Back to Blake.

Not quite yet. Her head wasn't near to accepting the weird way her body had reacted to his presence.

She gathered towels. She thought about Blake; how she could get him dry. His clothes were soaked. Towels?

Something more.

She hesitated, told herself she was stupid, fetched a bathrobe.

The dog stayed with her, sticking close, a feather-touch of contact.

This dog had done it hard, she thought. The Animal Welfare van had crashed over a week ago. Where had this dog been since then?

Mardie's heart wasn't hard at the best of times. She could feel it stretch right now.

'Yeah, I'm a sucker for dogs,' she told her. 'Especially beautiful dogs like you. But there must be some reason you were at the pound in the first place. Were you in for sheep-killing?'

That was the most common reason a farm dog ended up discarded. A dog got a taste for blood. It was tragic, but once a dog started killing sheep there was little that could be done.

Most farmers quietly put them down. If they were too attached, though, they'd take them to the pound, hoping some townie would take them on, someone with a contained yard with not a sheep in sight.

It hardly ever made for a happy ending. A working dog

wasn't meant to be contained. They pined, they made trouble for their new owners, they ended up being put down anyway.

So…she now had a stray dog, probably a sheep killer, and she had Blake Maddock.

A girl should have some protection.

A clap of thunder shook the house so loud the windows rattled.

She thought of Bounce under her bedclothes. Until the storm ended there was no way Bounce was moving.

She was on her own—but what else was new?

Having Blake Maddock in her kitchen was new.

You've faced worse than Blake Maddock, she told herself.

And…it was Blake. The thought made something inside her shiver, and it wasn't fear.

Hormones?

Nonsense. Hormones were for a teenage romance. Get over it. Be practical.

It was good advice. She took her armload of towels and her bathrobe, she took her courage in both hands—and went to see if she could follow it.

CHAPTER TWO

THE great thing about a wood-burning stove was that a power outage couldn't mess with it. Cutting wood was a pain, but Mardie had learned to enjoy it, and the stove more than paid for itself with comfort. In the small hours after a difficult lambing, when she was cold and wet, the fire was a warm, welcoming presence.

It was the heart of her home.

Blake was standing before it now. He'd put the kettle on the hob. He'd opened the toasting door so he could see the flames; so he could hold his hands out for warmth. He had his back to her.

He was so…large.

She'd known he'd become a doctor. Someone had been to a graduation ceremony in Sydney years back and had seen him.

She hadn't heard of him since. And now, here he was, big and handsome and rugged, wearing a dinner suit, a city doctor in city clothes.

She had a city doctor in her kitchen.

She had Blake in her kitchen.

See, there was the anomaly. Blake was from another life. Blake no longer fitted here, yet there was part of him that was…Blake.

And he didn't look like a city doctor, she thought as he

turned to face her. In truth, he looked more weathered than most farmers. He looked tanned and muscled, and the creases of his eyes were etched deep, as if he constantly faced harsh sun.

He also looked a bit…gaunt? That'd be the crash, she thought, but then she decided it looked more than that. She sensed deep-seated strain, and he looked too lean for health. He looked as if he might have been ill—or maybe he simply worked too hard.

City surgeon, making millions? More millions. She knew little about Blake's parents other than they'd been killed in a light plane crash when he was twelve, but she did know they were wealthy. His great-aunt had money, too.

Blake obviously had moved on in the same mould.

'I hear you're a doctor,' she said cautiously, and he nodded.

'Yes.'

'Congratulations.'

'On being a doctor?'

'Of course. You've cut your head. How bad is it?'

'It's nothing.'

'Have you hurt anything else?'

'No.'

'Promise?'

'Yes.'

'Let me check the cut for glass, then. Sit.'

'Still bossy?'

'Always.'

He sat.

He used to argue. Always.

Maybe he was hurt. Maybe he…

'I had six airbags,' he said. 'I was almost suffocated but not hurt. This has to be superficial. But I would be grateful if you could check.'

She checked. She filled a bowl with warm water, she

washed his face with care, she used the flashlight to check for glass.

It was an ugly scratch. There were a couple of metal slivers, embedded. She found tweezers, tugged them out. She put on antiseptic and a plaster.

Touching him was weird. Touching him felt…shivery.

Get over it. He was the one who should be shivery, not her. Concentrate on need.

'You need to get dry,' she said, trying to keep her voice steady. 'There's a bathrobe here that's wool and warm. Dry yourself and put it on.' Deep breath. 'I think you need to stay the night. I'd drive you into town but you've already proven it's not safe to be out. I don't see that you have a choice. You want to change now, while I towel the dog? Take a couple of candles upstairs. Same bedroom you always had. I keep the spare beds made up. You don't have a choice.'

How had that happened?

One minute he was deciding to turn back to Sydney. The next he was standing in Mardie's attic, hauling on her dressing gown.

No. Not hers. It was soft brown cashmere and it was huge. A man's.

Her father's?

He remembered Mardie's dad with huge regret. Bill was a big, genial countryman, deeply contented with his wife, his farm, his daughter. As kids, Blake and Mardie had trailed after him like two adoring puppies, helping, messing around, being with him.

Bill had died of a massive heart attack when Mardie was barely in her teens and he'd felt as gutted as Mardie. He'd felt little emotion when he'd been told his own parents were dead—he hadn't seen them for years—but Bill…

If this was Bill's bathrobe…

He smiled, remembering Bill, remembering this place as it had been.

Why had he never come back?

He knew why. Because of Mardie.

Mardie...

She'd grown up, of course she had, but she was still the same Mardie. She was short, blue-eyed, freckled and compact. Her honey-blonde curls were still tied into braids. And her eyes...

He'd always loved how they'd creased into laughter in an instant. Time had now etched those laughter lines to permanent.

Tonight she was wearing tattered jeans and an old woolly jumper. Bright red socks with a hole in one toe.

Years of tending sheep, of living on this farm meant she was wind-burned, sun-burned, cute as a button.

She was a farmer.

She could have been so much more...

No. It had been stupid to demand that of her fifteen years ago. It was stupid to think it now.

So get this over with, he told himself. Don't let your emotions get tangled up. Get in there, be courteous and thankful, accept her offer of a bed for the night, call for a tow truck first thing in the morning and get out of here. You've seen her. That was what you wanted. Now leave.

Because?

Because Banksia Bay seemed threatening, and Mardie seemed even more threatening. He didn't know why, but she was.

Or maybe he did. Maybe he was old enough to see it.

Mardie was comfort, fun, loving. She was a refuge, as she'd always been his refuge.

Mardie was all the things he could never let himself have.

* * *

What was keeping him? She towelled the little collie as dry as she could, encouraged her to lie in Bounce's dog basket, then started making toast.

The collie whined and headed back to her, once more just touching her knee.

She made toast and the dog kept contact all the time.

'What's wrong?' she asked, and offered her a piece of toast.

The dog didn't take it. As if she didn't see it was being held out.

She moved it a little closer.

The dog sniffed, sniffed again—and then delicately took it from Mardie's hand.

What the...?

She'd been working by candlelight. She flicked the flashlight back on and looked. She really looked. And in the better light...

No.

She plumped down on the kitchen chair and drew the dog to her.

'Oh, sweetheart. Oh, no.'

Blake walked back into the kitchen and stopped short.

The dog's head was resting on Mardie's knee. Tears were sliding unchecked down her face.

'Mardie...'

She looked up at him, and all the tragedy of the world was in her face.

'She's blind,' she whispered. 'She was tipped out of that van a week ago and she's blind. How's she ever survived?'

Blind.

Things fell into place.

The dog standing motionless in the road, not registering his oncoming car.

The dog touching him, staying by his side, following him here by touch.

The dog moving to Mardie, whose clothes would smell of farmyard, of the familiar, then not leaving her. Just touching.

'How do you know?' he asked, but already he knew it for truth.

'Look at her eyes.' She flicked on the flashlight.

He looked.

The dog's eyes were opaque, unfocused, unseeing. Cataracts covered both the eyes entirely.

She'd be seeing vague shapes, light and dark through thick white fog, he thought. Nothing more.

'It'll be why she was in the pound,' Mardie whispered. He'd walked back into the kitchen absurdly self-conscious of wearing a great woollen bathrobe but Mardie was oblivious to anything but the dog. 'She's only young. I'm guessing four at the most. And she's smart and so polite. She's skin and bone. She must be starving, yet she took the toast like a lady. Oh, sweetheart.'

She sniffed and sniffed again. She ran her fingers through her hair, a gesture he remembered, Mardie under stress. She'd obviously forgotten, though, that she'd tied her hair into braids. Her fingers caught one of the bands and her hair fell loose, a cascade of honey curls.

One braid in. The other free. Tear-stained, messy, freckled... She didn't care. She was totally oblivious.

Something kicked him, hard, deep inside. Something that hadn't kicked him for a long time.

'Let me see,' he said, more roughly than he intended. He knelt on the floor, cupping the dog's jaw in his hand, looking at her eyes.

The dog let him do as he willed. She was totally trusting, or maybe she'd gone past trust. Maybe she was at the point of: *Kill me now, nothing can get worse than this.*

Definitely cataracts.

If it was the same as humans... Cataracts sometimes came

with age. Sometimes they were caused by illness or injury. These, though…

'Sometimes they're genetic,' he said, thinking out loud. 'She seems a young, otherwise healthy dog.'

The dog let her head lie on his palm and sighed.

Mardie sniffed again.

'Years ago, one of my neighbours' old Labradors, Blacky, got cataracts,' she muttered. 'Roger said the cost of having them removed was too huge to consider. Blacky was a pet, though, old, fat and lazy at the best of times. He was content to live out the rest of his life in front of Roger's fire. But for a young working dog… If she can't work she'll be miserable, and useless to whoever owns her.'

She fingered the plastic collar.

The flashlight was still on. They read the collar together, Blake absurdly aware of honey-blonde curls tumbling to her shoulder only six inches away. Absurdly aware of a ragged sweater.

Mardie…

'She has a name.' Mardie seemed unaware of his distraction and Blake looked where she was looking. There was a number written in black on the collar, followed by rough script.

Bessie. Owner: Charlie Hunter.

'It's worse and worse,' Mardie said, and her face said it was.

'Charlie Hunter?'

'You must remember Charlie. He's a farmer up on the ridge. A nice old guy, keeps to himself, almost ninety. He used to be the best dog-trainer in the district. Brilliant. When he won All Australian Champion I made him…'

But then she faltered. Bit back what she'd been about to say.

'I guess…I guess whether I know him or not doesn't matter. But he had a stroke eight weeks ago and he's had to go into care. I'm guessing this is his dog.' She took a deep breath, and when she continued her voice cracked with emotion. 'So this is Bessie. He kept her even though she was blind, and when he could no longer keep her he put her in the pound. I wouldn't have thought… It would have been kinder to put her down.'

And she rose and walked out of the room.

Bessie sniffed his hand and he patted her, stroking her silky coat. The kettle whistled on the stove.

The roof was leaking in the corner, into a bucket. A steady trickle. The bucket was almost full.

He took a candle and checked the living room, the matching corner. Another bucket.

The way they were filling, it'd be a twenty-minute roster to empty them, all night.

He made tea and then Mardie was back, with another collie by her side. Bigger. Younger. Having to be towed.

'Bounce,' she said sternly, hauling him into the room whether he liked it or not. 'Get over the thunder. You're needed. Meet Bessie.'

Bounce was clearly cowed by the storm. Another low rumble filled the night. His ears flattened and he whimpered.

Bessie whimpered back.

Bounce's ears forgot about flattening. Another dog, in his kitchen? This clearly took precedence over thunder. He launched himself forward, stopping abruptly two inches from Bessie's nose. He sniffed.

Bessie sniffed back.

The procedure was repeated from different viewpoints.

Bounce gave his tail a cautious wag.

'Basket,' Mardie said.

At the side of the woodstove was an ancient dog basket. There'd been dogs in that basket ever since Blake could remember. There were never less than three. He'd been vaguely surprised not to see dogs in there tonight.

The family was down to one dog?

'Basket,' Mardie said again. Bounce gave her a *Must I?* look but turned and headed where he was meant to go.

Bessie went too, just touching.

Bounce turned in two circles, sighed, flopped.

Bessie flopped, too. Closed her eyes. Was asleep in an instant.

Bounce stared up at Mardie, doubtful as to this new order.

'Stay,' Mardie said gently, and Bounce sighed again, but he wriggled until his body was curved around Bessie's. He settled.

'That's great,' Blake said, feeling immeasurably cheered. 'Another dog...they have ways of figuring they can trust.'

'They'll both relax,' Mardie said. 'Bounce wasn't finding me the least bit reassuring against the gods of thunder but an older one who's not scared is just what he needs.'

'And tomorrow?'

'Tomorrow I'll call Henrietta, who runs the pound,' she said bleakly, sitting back down at the table. Hauling her mug of tea close and holding it, as if needing the comfort of its warmth. 'But one step at a time. Would you like toast before bed?'

She was suddenly businesslike. Brisk. Putting emotion aside.

There were still tracks of tears on her cheeks.

He found her absurdly...or not absurdly...

'I don't need anything to eat,' he said, a bit too abruptly. 'I've just had a reunion dinner.'

'So you have. You're sure your head's okay?'

'It's fine. Thank you.' She was seated right by him. So close... Instinctively he reached out to touch her hand. It was a gesture of gratitude, nothing more.

She flinched.

It was as much as he could do not to flinch in return.

'I'm staying up to eat toast,' she said, carefully focusing

on her mug of tea and not him. 'Sleep well. There's a bit to face in the morning, so get some rest.'

'Mardie?'

She did look at him then, with all the distrust in the world. His heart twisted.

'When I left...I never meant to hurt you,' he said.

'You did hurt me,' she said, flat and definite. The emotion of that instinctive hug was gone; remembered hurt was back. 'I wrote to you. I worried about you. You never wrote back.'

'I needed...to protect myself.'

'Then that's all right,' she said stiffly. 'All explained.'

'I was a kid. I was stupid, not to keep in contact with my best friend.'

'We were teenagers,' she conceded. 'Sensitivity isn't a teenager's strong suit. Forget it. Go to bed.'

'Sensitive or not, I've regretted it. More and more as I grew older.'

'It doesn't matter.'

'It did to me. It does. I am sorry. That's why I came tonight. I wanted to see you. It's what I wanted to say.' And before he could think it through—because if he had he never would have done it—he stooped and he kissed her. His kiss was light, a brush of his mouth against her forehead. It was a kiss given because he couldn't bear not to. A kiss of apology.

It was a dumb gesture. She pulled away as if he burned.

'That's enough of sorry,' she told him brusquely, harshly. 'It was all a long time ago. It doesn't matter any more; just go.'

'Are you planning on bucket-emptying all night?'

She sighed. Looked at the buckets. Didn't look at him. 'They'll be okay.'

'They'll flood.'

She'd been thinking that, in the fraction of her mind that wasn't taken up by him. An hour ago the leak had been a drip.

The drip was becoming a trickle and the trickle was threatening to turn to a gush.

'I'm sure it'll be fine.' Some things weren't worth worrying about. No way was she getting up on the roof in this weather.

'It'll be the corner of the roof, where the spouts meet,' he said. 'The water's banking up; there's too much for the drainpipe to cope with.'

'How do you know?'

'I've coped with more than floods over the last few years. Once upon a time your dad let me up on the roof with him. I can remember the set-up, and I know down-pipes.'

'You understand plumbing?' She was incredulous.

He grinned. 'Hey, I'm a doctor. Plumbing's half my med training. Plus my work has been practical in more ways than one. So now, not only am I offering my professional opinion, I'm proposing surgery. Though I'll need to put my dinner suit back on. There's no way I'm getting Bill's robe wet.'

She wasn't listening to the end of his statement. She was too intent on the first. 'You can't get on the roof. Are you out of your mind? Have you seen the lightning?'

'I have,' he agreed, grateful that here was something concrete he could do, something to lessen the emotion. 'It's sheet lightning, not fork. Fork's bad. Sheet's not great but we also have trees, much taller than the house. Plus there's two chimneys, both of which would be hit before the house itself. I'm not proposing to stand on the roof acting as a lightning conductor. I'm proposing to stick a ladder against the corner of the house while you hold the bottom, then climb up and disengage the down-pipe. I might need a hacksaw. Do you have a hacksaw?'

'I…might,' she said, flabbergasted.

'Excellent. With just a hole instead of a pipe, the water'll stop banking up under the eaves.'

'How do you know?' she said, suspicious, and he grinned.

'Trust me, I'm a doctor.'

She didn't grin back. 'You'd go outside again—into the storm?' She was still hornswoggled. 'Plus you have a lump the size of an egg on your head.'

'Hero material, that's me,' he said, trying to make her smile. 'But I'm not too heroic. The lump's already subsiding and I know what I'm doing. But I do need my sidekick—that'd be you in your sou'wester.'

'I wouldn't need to get up all night,' she said, dazed.

'There's my board and lodging paid for. What about it, Mardie? Deal?'

She struggled to shut her mouth. Stop being flabbergasted. 'You're proposing we brave the tempest?' she managed. 'With a ladder? I don't mind a bit of rain. Rainstorms are when most of my lambs seem to be born. But you… You'll need to put that disgusting dinner suit on again.'

'It's not disgusting.'

'If it's not yet, it soon will be,' she said darkly. 'But this is an offer I'm not refusing. Okay, Superman, you're on.'

He fixed the leak, by the simple expedient of climbing the ladder, hacking the drainpipe out of the spout, clearing the worst of the banked-up leaf litter and letting the water gush free. He even managed to do it so water didn't land on Mardie's head as she held the ladder below. It seemed simple, except she couldn't have done it. Balance in the rain and handle a hacksaw as if accustomed to it. Balance while not noticing the lightning.

He was steady and sure and fast.

She felt…

She felt…

She had no idea how she felt.

He came down the ladder. Brushed against her, which made her feel…as if she didn't know how she felt. Grinned, a triumphant small-boy grin she remembered. 'Flood averted,' he said. 'Much better than a finger in the dyke, don't you think?'

'Much,' she said faintly, because she couldn't think of anything else to say.

When had he got so big?

When had he got so...male?

They stowed the ladder, they came back inside and he dripped in the hall.

'Would you...' she started and then she stopped. She simply didn't know what to say next.

'Would I like another towel? Yes, I would. And then bed.'

'I... Thank you.'

'Enough of the thank yous. Let's call it quits.' He touched her lightly on her cheek—and she flinched and his smile died.

She got him his towel. He nodded his thanks and headed straight for bed. Up to the attic where he'd stayed when he was a kid.

She headed back to the kitchen. She'd told him she was staying up to eat toast.

She'd lied.

She was staying up to think about Blake.

Blake Maddock was in her attic.

Blake Maddock had fixed her plumbing. Blake Maddock had kissed her.

Blake Maddock had touched her cheek, a gesture of farewell, and her cheek still burned.

For this was a new Blake Maddock; the grown-up version. He was a guy who'd pulled away her flooding down-pipes as if he coped with manual labour every day of his life.

That was what he looked like.

Whatever he'd been doing for the past fifteen years, it hadn't made him soft. He was lean—almost too lean—but his muscles made up for it. And his body... As he'd come back down the ladder, his soaked clothes clinging, he'd looked... he'd looked...

A girl shouldn't think how he'd looked.

And he'd kissed her.

So…what? He'd kissed her for the first time when she was six years old and she'd given him her sandwich. She'd giggled and her friends had said 'kissy kissy'. They'd all giggled then. She and Blake were best of friends.

Not any more. They weren't even minor friends. Friends would have sat up for an hour or so, catching up on what had happened through the years.

He didn't want to catch up. He was stuck here because his car had crashed. He'd fixed her down-pipe because he felt sorry for her. He wanted to get the night over and get back to Sydney.

So why had he kissed her?'

'Because he's arrogant and he has more money than anyone has a right to. He thinks he's aristocracy.' She said it out loud but it didn't make sense.

He'd never acted rich. All the time she'd known him, he acted as if his family's money was something he didn't want to know about.

He never talked about his parents, then or now. Everything she knew, she knew from scant town gossip.

Tonight…she should have asked what he'd been doing. She'd assumed he was a city doctor, but he looked so weathered…he must have been doing something else.

Neither had asked the important questions. Neither had told.

She should have told him her mother wasn't here. He could have slept in the front bedroom.

Would he be able to sleep in the tiny attic bed?

It didn't matter, she told herself, sticking bread in the toaster without thinking. Their friendship was over. She hadn't seen him for fifteen years and after tonight she wouldn't see him again.

She shouldn't mind.

Quite suddenly, quite fiercely, she minded.

What would her life be if she'd gone to Sydney with him?

Maybe she'd be a doctor's wife. A rich doctor's wife. They'd have a gorgeous house, a couple of kids, piano lessons, mid-week tennis. Society functions. Ladies' lunches.

Um…how about that for a stereotype?

She could have gone to university as he'd wanted her to. She'd been smart enough. Maybe she could have been a doctor, too.

A doctor? Her favourite subject at school was art, and she still remembered the adolescent Blake's disparagement. 'It's all right for a hobby but not for a career.'

He'd had ambition. She didn't, or not ambition as he saw it. She'd never wanted to leave Banksia Bay.

Apart from Blake. She'd wanted, desperately, to go wherever Blake went.

At school he'd been quiet about his future, telling no one, even hugging his desire to study medicine to himself. He kept lots of things to himself. Even to her, his best of friends, he'd seldom talked of his family, his future, or his past. Maybe that was wise. His family's wealth made him different from most kids in Banksia Bay. The eccentricity of his great-aunt made him different. The fact that he had fabulously wealthy parents who never came near made him really different.

He was still…different.

He probably had a wife, she thought suddenly. He might even have cute, piano-playing kids.

He wasn't wearing a wedding ring. She'd noticed.

'Don't go there,' she told herself, and ate the toast without thinking about it.

Bounce opened one eye and watched with hope. She gave him a crust, then offered another to Bessie, but Bessie didn't stir.

She was a smaller dog than Bounce. Sweet.

Blind.

'Don't think it,' she told herself, but she knew she was thinking it.

She couldn't. It'd be cruel to keep a blind working dog. It'd be sentimentality at its worst.

'And it's not as if there's any spare money to spend on operations.' She was still talking out loud. 'Even if it's possible.'

A thunderclap rolled across the night and made her shudder. Instead of heading behind her legs, Bounce simply nestled closer to Bessie.

Bounce had a new best friend.

Which left her alone.

Bed. Alone. Without even Bounce.

'That's a dumb, sad thing to think,' she told herself. 'Ooh, who's feeling sorry for herself? Go to bed and enjoy listening to the thunder. And don't keep thinking of Blake. He's nothing to do with you and he's out of here, first thing in the morning.'

He should have sat up and talked.

He lay in the dark and counted bruises to distract himself. The crash hadn't left him completely unscathed. His head ached. Something had thumped his shoulder and that ached, too.

He'd been barely civil downstairs. He hadn't asked anything of her life for the past fifteen years. How dumb was that?

She'd think he was just using her.

He *was* using her. This was the closest place to stay out of the storm. Even if they'd been strangers he would have asked for shelter, and she might have been kind enough to say yes.

Of course she would. This was Mardie, still feeling sorry for strays after all these years.

What had she been doing all this time? Married? He should have looked for a ring.

Surely not. A husband would have made himself obvious.

Her mother? Etta hadn't appeared either, but Etta had suffered from appalling arthritis fifteen years back. She'd occasionally been bed-ridden even then. How was she now?

He should have asked.

He should have asked lots of things.

Once upon a time he'd known all there was to know about Mardie. They'd been lone children on adjoining farms. When his parents had sent him here, seven years old, deeply traumatised, he'd missed his twin as if part of him had been ripped away. Mardie had helped fill that appalling void. They'd spent their childhood together. Best friends.

And then... Six months before his final exams he'd suddenly seen Mardie differently.

Theirs had been a fumbling teenage love affair, as painful as it was sweet. But it meant, for the first time, he saw a possibility for sharing the load into the future, of having someone by him as he carried his burden of guilt and grief.

How unfair was that? He'd never even explained—how could he? *Help me make up for my brother's life?*

He'd said simply, 'Follow me to Sydney,' and she'd said no.

'Write,' she'd said.

He'd thought at first that he could, but what he hadn't realised was how much it hurt. Those first months in a huge, anonymous university college, away from anyone he knew... Losing Mardie... It had been like losing Robbie all over again.

But he had to leave. Banksia Bay was where he'd been dumped. It had become a refuge but he'd always known he had to leave.

'Stay there until we all forget,' his father had said. Even at seventeen he'd known forgetting was never going to happen. Staying in Banskia Bay seemed like a long, continuous betrayal of memory.

So he had to leave, but if he'd phoned Mardie, if he'd heard her voice, if he'd made any contact at all, then he risked crumbling. And how could he do that?

Robbie, his ghost, his shadow, was driving him.

Behind Robbie… His parents, running through inherited money as if it was water, squandering their lives, losing Robbie in the process. Consciously forgetting their son.

His great-aunt, floundering after an ill-advised love affair, locking herself away in Banksia Bay, as far from what she thought of as civilisation as she could get, using her inheritance as a shield from the world. Consciously forgetting her lover.

So many lives, wasted. Including Robbie's.

For Robbie's sake, the squandering would stop. The forgetting would stop.

So he'd decided that contacting Mardie would simply keep the wound open. Then, by the time he was settled, by the time the ache eased, it seemed too late to rekindle friendship. He'd burned his bridges, and now he had to pay the price.

The price was that tonight she'd welcomed him almost as a stranger. He'd kissed her and she'd backed away. He'd touched her and she'd flinched. And he'd gone to bed without even asking about her mother.

They'd have time to talk in the morning, he thought. He'd ask…and then he'd leave.

Again.

He stirred uneasily. The spare bed always had been too small, too hard. He ached.

The storm kept on, unabated.

He lay awake and thought of Mardie. Of a life long past.

Of a seventeen-year-old who was desperate to save the world, to do *something*, but who wanted to carry Mardie with him.

Why remember it now? Theirs was a childhood friendship, faded to nothing. He shouldn't have come.

It was just…the invitation to the reunion had seemed almost meant. He wasn't sure why he'd kept thinking of Mardie during this last long illness, but he had.

The Mardie of his childhood.

The problem was, he decided as he drifted towards sleep, it wasn't the Mardie of years ago he was thinking of now. It was the Mardie of now. Mardie hugging him joyously in that first instinctive burst of surprised welcome. Mardie in her vast sou'wester, holding the ladder as if this was the sort of work she did every day of the week. Mardie, as she was, but a thousandfold more.

Why had he returned?

Sleep was nowhere.

The night had no answers, and neither did he.

CHAPTER THREE

BLAKE finally slept—and he woke to the sound of singing.

For a moment he thought he was dreaming. He was in a tiny attic room. Whitewashed walls. A narrow bed.

For that instant he was back in his childhood, and then he was wide awake. The events of the night before flooded back.

Mardie was outside, somewhere below his bedroom window. Singing.

He glanced at his watch. Silly o'clock.

He swung himself out of bed and winced. Yes, the airbags had saved him from injury but he was still battered.

He also still suffered aches from illness. Haemorrhagic dengue did that to you. He stretched cautiously. Ouch.

The singing went on. It was something operatic, ridiculous, sung at the top of her lungs. Mardie at full caterwaul.

He found himself grinning, remembering early grade school. The whole school had been learning Christmas carols for the annual concert. An ambitious music teacher had listened to each child in turn. Divided them into sections. Soprano, alto, baritone, tenor.

She'd listened to Mardie, grimaced and given her a section of her own.

'You can be the drum,' Miss Watson had decreed. 'Stay at the back and boom along to the beat. Just sing "Pum Pum Pum Pum Pum."'

But what Mardie lacked in talent she made up for in enthusiasm. The night of the school concert, Mardie's ear-shattering "Pums" had practically drowned out the choir, and the audience had dissolved into delighted laughter.

Mardie had laughed as well.

He grinned at the memory, his aches receding as he pulled open the shutters and looked down.

She was milking the cow. One cow. This was sheep country, not dairy. She'd be milking for personal use.

Or not. One cow made a lot of milk.

Who was living in this house with her?

The house was silent. The storm of the night before was past. The early-morning sun was glittering on the wet paddocks.

Mardie was sitting in the little open shed at the back gate, calmly milking the cow in the wooden bail he remembered climbing on as a child.

This place was a time warp, he thought. All the things he'd done in the past fifteen years...

He'd seen the world. His work in Africa...

She'd stayed home and milked the cow.

'Rather than stand and stare, make yourself useful,' she yelled up at him. 'There's bacon in the fridge. Start cooking. I'll be inside in five minutes.'

Had he been so obvious?

'Is there anyone else home?' he yelled back.

'No.' Short and to the point. 'Except the dogs and they're not moving. I think they're in love.'

'Mardie...'

'Bacon,' she yelled. 'I'd like four rashers, two tomatoes, four slices of toast and I'll cook my own eggs when I get in. Or you can milk the cow. Take your pick. By the way, the pool of water under the downpipe's practically a swimming pool. If you hadn't diverted it, it'd be in my house. You deserve four rashers as well.'

* * *

His dinner suit was still sodden. Of course. Clothes were an issue. Why hadn't he brought spares? Feeling…weird…he donned Bill's bathrobe again and headed downstairs.

The kitchen was warm and welcoming and smelled of damp dog. Or a bit more. Bessie's week of being a stray had left her distinctly on the nose. But if there was one thing Blake's work in Africa had equipped him for, it was working with smells. He might bathe her before he left, he thought.

Or maybe not. Maybe he should leave fast.

Depending on Mardie.

Both dogs rose as he entered, heading out of their basket to greet him. Bessie came side by side with Bounce. Just touching. She'd learned this mechanism to cope, he thought—finding something trustworthy and sticking like glue.

She touched his hand with her wet nose and he felt his gut twist.

A blind working dog…

Don't get involved, he told himself, but he already was. He was thinking of bathing her but he was thinking much more.

Breakfast first.

He knew this place backwards. Little had changed. The kitchen had been repainted, though. Sea blue. Nice. The big old woodstove was still the centrepiece.

There were a couple of extraordinary enamelled paintings on either side. Abstract. They looked like wildfire under glass. Even when the woodstove wasn't lit, these paintings would give warmth to the room, he thought. Mardie always did have an eye for good art.

Breakfast.

The vast frying pan, black with age, seemed an old friend. The bacon was a slab rather than pre-cut rashers, just like it'd always been when he stayed here as a kid. He cut it thick, tossed rashers into the pan, and dog smell was immediately replaced by cooking bacon.

The dogs wiggled with hope, and he cut more. It was a special morning. Bacon all round.

He was halfway through making toast when Mardie appeared. She was wearing another ancient sweater with holes in the elbows. She'd pulled her gumboots off at the door and her feet were covered with bright yellow socks. No holes this morning. Sartorial elegance at its finest.

She'd done her hair, braiding it and coiling it high. It made her look a little more sophisticated than last night, but not much. Nothing could ever make this woman sophisticated, he thought. She was carrying a bucket of milk, the quintessential dairymaid. She looked…

Incredibly sexy.

That was a dumb thing to think. Since when had faded jeans, torn sweater and a bucket of milk made a woman sexy?

But there was no denying, Mardie was…sexy.

And it seemed the admiration worked both ways. 'I'm glad you've put on the bathrobe,' she said as she heaved her bucket onto the bench. 'Have you been working out? I can't remember all those muscles. Standing at the attic window showing them off…I would have thought a bit of modesty would be appropriate.' Then, as he started to feel discomfited, she grinned. 'I know. It's bad manners to comment, but manners were never my forte. And while I'm commenting… You're too thin. You want a glass of milk? Guaranteed non-pasteurised, non-homogenised, organic, still warm from its own personal milk heater, Clarabelle Cow.'

She dipped a ladle into the bucket and poured two big glasses. Handed him one.

How long since he'd drunk milk straight from the cow?

He thought of the hospital food he'd endured over the past awful weeks. Thought he should have just come here.

That was a bad idea.

He put down the glass and she smiled. 'Milk moustache,' she said and handed him a tissue. 'Nothing changes.'

Something had. They used to wipe each other's milk moustaches. That had started when they were knee high to a grasshopper. The fact that she'd handed him a tissue…

Now they were practically strangers.

It behoved a man to remember it.

'Why the cow? Can you drink a bucket a day?' he asked.

'I make cheese with a friend. Lorraine's a local potter—we help each other in all sorts of ways and we make cheese on the side. We have one cow each. It works well because if either of us is busy we do the other's milking. And we're good. We sell it at our farmer's market. You have no idea how much we can charge, and it's fun.'

Fun. For some reason the word threw him.

Mardie, with her milk moustache, having fun.

'How long have you been up?' he asked, moving on with an effort.

'Dawn. I went round the sheep to make sure none got hit by lightning, but the Cyprus hedge is a great shelter and they're fine. The gum's down across the drive, though. You had to go round it last night?'

'Yeah.' His mud-covered shoes on the veranda testified to the scrambling he'd had to do to get here.

'I'll get the chainsaw onto it. That's my after-breakfast job. Oh, and I believe your car's a write-off.'

'You've seen it?'

'I've seen it,' she said grimly. 'How fast were you going?'

'Obviously too fast.'

'You're so lucky you're not dead.'

And there was something about the way she said it… The lightness suddenly disappeared. Her words were flat, with a faint tremor beneath.

There was something about the way her face changed.

He knew this woman. He hadn't seen her for fifteen years but he knew…

'Who else has been killed in a car crash?' he asked, and it was a question and a statement all in one.

'I...' She stopped. She shook her head but he knew her denial was a lie.

'Your mother?' He felt sick. *He should have asked.*

'My mum's in Banksia Bay Nursing Home.' She concentrated on fetching eggs from the pantry, refusing to return to car wrecks. 'Her arthritis cripples her. I bring her out here whenever I can. She sits on the veranda in the sun and tells me all the things I'm doing wrong.' She smiled again then, starting to crack eggs into the pan. Moving on. And he couldn't push. *He had no right.*

'But you know something?' she said, still inexorably changing the subject. 'She's happy. She doesn't need to stay here. All these years we fought to keep her independent, she finally gave in and now she's surrounded by friends. She plays bridge, she watches old movies, she reads. She doesn't need her daughter to do the humiliating things. She comes out here and enjoys the farm but she's always ready to go back to her comfy bedroom with her music and her books and the local nurses who make her feel loved. I don't feel bad about it at all.'

'So you're here completely by yourself?'

There was a moment's hesitation. Then... 'Yes.' It was almost defiant.

'You should have gone to university.' It was an explosion.

She paused, mid egg break. Stiffened. Then she calmly went on breaking eggs. Four. She scooped bacon fat over them so they cooked sunny-side up. Slid them onto two plates. Sat at the table and loaded her plate with bacon.

'I've never regretted it,' she said at last. 'Not for a moment.'

'Look at you.' Why was he feeling so angry? Why was he feeling...that it had all been a waste? It wasn't fair to attack her, her lifestyle, but...the idea that she'd been *mouldering* here was suddenly killing him. 'I go away for fifteen years,

I get myself a medical degree, a career. I've done so much. And you...'

'Have you been happy?'

'Happiness isn't the point.'

'What else is the point?' she demanded, buttering toast. 'My mother's arthritis started when she was thirty. When she was thirty-eight she lost her husband. Yet she's happy. She had the choice. Miserable or happy. She chose happy. She still chooses happy. Pass the marmalade, please.'

'What did she do with her life?'

'She made us all happy,' she snapped. 'Including you. Don't you dare say that's a waste. Marmalade!'

'Where are you putting all this?' She was about five feet two. She was little and wiry and compact. She was eating enough to keep him going for a full day.

'Work makes you hungry,' she said evenly, and her anger had been carefully and obviously put away. 'You've been lying in bed letting your calories sink languorously anywhere they want. My calories have been bouncing all the way down to the bottom paddock on the tractor, into the bails to milk Clarabelle, over to see your car and the ruined tree, and they're all used up. Speaking of your car...' She glanced at her watch. 'I'll ring Raff, the local cop, at eight. And Henrietta.'

'Henrietta?'

'The lady who runs the pound.'

'No.'

It was an explosion, and the word stopped them both short.

Mardie paused, her bacon midway to her mouth. She gazed at him, calm and direct. 'No?'

From their basket, the two dogs watched. Or one dog watched and the other watched by proxy. Bounce had been declared Bessie's eyes.

'No?' she said cautiously. 'Are you offering her a home?'

'I can't.' That was practically an explosion, too.

'Neither can I.' She met his gaze square on. Knew what he was asking. Rejected it. 'Don't ask it of me.'

He needed to make some phone calls before he talked about the next option. He needed to know his facts. But for now... 'Why not?' he asked.

'She's a working dog. Look at her. She's beautiful, young, energetic, aching to run. She's bred to work. I've seen injured working dogs before. Without their work, they pine. Look at how thin she is. Charlie Hunter is a kind old man and he would have loved her to bits. He'll have fed her whatever she'll take. When he went into the nursing home he'll have handed her over to Henrietta at the pound, and Hen loves dogs. She'll have hand fed her if that's what it took to get her to eat. But she's still stick-thin. I know a depressed dog when I see one. She's blind and she's miserable.'

'So you'd put her down?'

'Like it's *my* decision?' She glared. 'That's unfair and you know it. But as for keeping her... Bounce would be out every day with me, working the sheep. He'd come home and Bessie would smell him, would know what we'd been doing. Border collies have arguably the highest IQ in the animal kingdom. They're not content to be lapdogs. It won't be safe for me to have her where sheep might kick her, where blind doesn't work. She's not meant to spend the rest of her life in a basket by the fire and I won't do it to her.'

'Cataracts are removable.'

'Maybe.' She spread marmalade on a second piece of toast, looked at it and then set it aside. 'I read my veterinary guide after you went to bed last night. Cataract operations in dogs are problematic. There's a high chance of failure and the cost per eye is astronomical. I couldn't even think of going there. Putting her though that...'

'But if you wanted her...'

'You found her,' she said, and her voice was back to harsh. 'She could never stay with me.'

'What's the difference between staying in a city apartment while you work all day, or staying by herself here?'

'I don't work in Australia,' he said.

'You don't work in Sydney?'

'My great-aunt had an apartment there. I'm clearing it out. From now on I'll be based in California. I really can't take on a dog. But I didn't mean to make you responsible.'

'But you did,' she said, suddenly savage. 'You're making me feel all sorts of things I don't want to feel.'

He raked his hair. 'I'm sorry.'

'Good. Excellent, in fact. Let's get you out of here.'

That was surely the best option. He glanced down at his bathrobe. Winced. Thought about his still-soggy dinner suit.

She'd followed his glance. 'I'll run into town when the shops open and buy what you need.'

'I need to get back to Sydney.'

'There's a bus this afternoon.'

'I don't...'

'Want to use the bus? You have no choice. Otherwise you're stuck here for the weekend and this house is too small. You know it is. Now, if you'll excuse me, I have work to do.'

'What needs doing?'

'I told you. I need to attack the tree across the drive with the chainsaw. Otherwise I can't get into town to get you clothes. I also need to move the sheep back into the outer paddocks. The Cyprus run's restricted—it's my safe paddock but there's not much feed. I either have to move them or hand feed them. So if you'll excuse me... Every minute you keep me here is a minute more before I can run into town to get clothes.'

'You expect me to sit in your father's bathrobe while you work?'

She stilled. 'My father's bathrobe?'

'I assumed...'

'Don't assume,' she snapped. 'My father never wore a bath-robe in his life.'

'Whose…?'

'Stay out of it.' Her anger was palpable. Any minute she'd throw something at him.

'Mardie, I need to help you,' he said, feeling his way through what seemed a minefield.

'You can help by staying out of my way.'

He rose, angry himself. 'I'm not useless.'

'You're useless in a bathrobe or a dinner suit.'

'I did fix the spouting.'

She glowered. 'So you did. I'm trying to remember it.'

'Are you punishing me for walking away fifteen years ago?'

Whoa. There was a moment's deathly silence. Her face lost colour. She closed her eyes and when she opened them something had changed. Anger had been replaced with pure ice.

'Are you out of your mind?' she demanded, speaking slowly, each syllable dripping with frost. 'You think I've been longing for you for fifteen years? Doing nothing? Grazing a few sheep, pining after my long-lost love, playing lovelorn little hayseed?'

'I didn't say…'

'You didn't have to say. What you're thinking is like a huge placard over your head.'

'All I said was that it was a waste…'

'To stay here? To live where I love to live?'

'A hundred sheep…'

'I'm a craft therapist, Blake Maddock.' She was practi-cally yelling. 'And an artist. I did my training part-time, an art course in Whale Cove, going back and forth for almost four years. I work in the local nursing home, organising out-ings, craft, music, fun. I also practice my art and I'm good. It gives me huge pleasure, and I'm starting to sell. I've sold off acreage because I can't run this farm as a full-time commitment but I still love it. My sheep make me happy. I love my work in the nursing home. I make the best cheese in the district. My mum still loves coming out here. I don't earn enough for luxury but I love everything about my life. And in case you think I've been pining for you… You think you're wearing my dad's bathrobe? I bought that for Hugh. For my husband. Hugh was killed in a car accident two years ago, the week before Christmas, the week before I gave it to him. For some reason I kept it and I loved it. So you're standing there in my husband's bathrobe, accusing me of having no life, of having lived in a time warp since you left, of doing nothing. And you kissed me last night like you were doing me a favour!'

There was no *practically yelling* about it. The last sentence was truly a blast. The dogs backed to the far end of the basket and cringed.

Blake felt like doing exactly the same.

'Mardie…'

'I'm not listening to another word. If I listen to any more, you risk getting a bucket of milk thrown at you. I'm going out now. I'm going to cut the tree away from the driveway and I'm moving sheep. Then I'm going to drive into town, fetch you some clothes that aren't Hugh's and buy you a bus ticket. I believe it leaves at two. I'll drive you to the bus station and it'll be pure pleasure to see the back of you. It was lovely to see you but now it'll be lovely to see you go. So now… Take care of the dogs while I'm out. And thanks for cooking the bacon. I'd eat some more but I feel like choking.'

She stomped out of the kitchen. Bounce leaped after her and she slammed the door.

He was left with Bessie.

He was left with what he'd done.

* * *

Bessie whimpered, nosed her way across to him and lay her head on his knee.

The little collie was doing it for her own need, not his, he told himself, but he took comfort anyway as she rubbed her head under his palm.

Mardie was a widow. She'd trained as a craft therapist.

Fifteen years and he knew nothing of anything. It was a great black hole.

He should have kept in touch.

Walking away from Banksia Bay had been a no-brainer. From the moment Robbie died he knew he'd have to do something. He remembered the announcement of his final-year marks, the letter offering him a place at medical school and the relief of finally knowing he had a plan.

But then he remembered telling Mardie and watching her face pale as it had paled a few moments ago.

He'd been exuberant, exultant. 'I'm going to Sydney. I can finally do something with my life.'

He glanced out of the window at the rain-washed world, at the undulating paddocks, the vast, spreading gums lining the driveway, the shimmer of the sea in the distance.

He and Mardie had spent a magical childhood in this place. Wandering the farm, the beaches, the harbour. Surfing, rabbiting, messing round with boats, nothing to contain them.

But he needed to work. In Africa he'd made a difference. No more.

He glanced out of the window again. Mardie was heading up the drive on the tractor, towards the shattered tree. Chainsaw on the back. Bounce running along behind.

A husband, dead. A mother cared for.

A wasted life?

It was unfair. He needed to apologise.

He already had. There was nothing more to be said. She wanted him to leave.

He couldn't leave yet. He'd work with her one last time.

He'd make amends if he could.

Bessie stirred on his knee, her blind eyes staring at nothing, white clouds of fog.

'Maybe we're both blind,' he told her.

Me, me, me. Wrong attitude. To be feeling sorry for himself when this dog was in such need.

Self-pity helped no one. He needed to help Mardie. He needed to sort the fate of Bessie. He needed to make some phone calls.

And then he needed to leave.

CHAPTER FOUR

THE tree had spilt straight down the middle. The scorch marks from the lightning formed a vicious slash down the side of the trunk still standing and the ground around the base was scorched black.

She loved the trees down the driveway, a sentinel of mighty gums a hundred years old.

She felt like crying.

Not just for the tree.

What was he doing, walking into her life again with his stupid, hurtful judgements? What crazy twist of fate had him crash his car where hers was the closest house?

Seeing him stand in her kitchen…in the bathrobe she'd bought for Hugh…

It made her feel tired and old and ill.

And also immeasurably sad. Her first sensation on seeing him again had been joy. Then, as she'd stood in the rain last night, holding the ladder while he fought her drainpipe, the joy had turned to something else. Something inexplicable.

A resurrection of what she'd once felt, or something more?

It didn't matter what she'd felt. She didn't need his judgement.

Work was her salvation. If she worked hard enough she didn't have to think. This tree would take weeks to clear, but she'd do enough now to clear the drive.

She attacked the smaller branches first, slicing them free and dragging them clear. After chopping the main branches for firewood, she'd be left with a pile of leaf litter. She'd use it eventually for mulch, but first she had to get it into a clear space so at the height of summer she didn't risk fire as it rotted and heated.

It was heavy work, heaving branches onto the trailer on the back of the tractor, but work was what she needed to defuse anger.

Work had always been her salvation. When her mother grew sicker. When Hugh died.

When Blake left.

How could she put Blake leaving alongside her grief for her mother, for Hugh?

She'd been sixteen. It couldn't have hurt as much.

She still remembered it though. Blake walking away.

She wanted to cry.

She didn't.

It was just…him walking back. Reminding her of what she'd lost.

She hadn't lost anything. She especially hadn't lost Blake. She'd never had him.

The chainsaw sliced through a protruding branch. She stepped back smartly as it crashed from the broken trunk.

It was hauled away before it hit the ground.

She turned, and Blake was there.

He was back in his dinner suit. Or most of his dinner suit. Trousers and shirt and shoes. His trousers were still soaked. His gorgeous dress shoes were muddy. His white shirt was damp, the top buttons were undone and the sleeves were rolled up. Everything clung.

Don't look. He made her feel…

Don't feel.

He grabbed the branch and dragged it across to the trailer.

'You'll ruin your suit,' she managed.

'I can afford it.'

Of course he could. Money had never been an issue.

The old stories seeped back. Miss Maddock, Blake's great-aunt. She'd arrived here in her thirties, so gossip said, cashed up, buying the lonely house out on the headland, doing it up almost as a mansion, but seeing no one. There was money to pay for upkeep, money to keep her isolated, money enough to snub the district, take a shopping trip to Sydney once a month, be as eccentric as she liked.

Mardie was too young to remember when Blake arrived but she knew the gossip about that, too. 'His mother's ill. His parents have more money than they know what to do with. The aunt's agreed to look after him until his mum gets better, heaven help him.'

Then, as he was about to finish junior school, more gossip. 'They're dead in a plane cash in Italy. Blake'll have to stay on with the old lady. Word is the parents were really rich. It's in trust for the kid. Though how he can use it, stuck here with her…'

The town heard a little about the plane crash, learned Blake's father was a wealthy gambler who spent his life between casinos, learned his mother had been 'ill' for a long time, learned nothing else. The aunt shut up and told the town to mind its own business.

Past history. She hauled her thoughts back to now.

Don't feel.

She cut the chainsaw motor and the silence stunned her. 'Thank you,' she said.

'It's the least I can do,' he said shortly, heaving the branch with a strength that put hers in the shade. 'After offending you just about every way I can think of, I need to make amends. You want me to keep going with this while you move the sheep?'

'Chainsawing's a skill.'

'Hey, I'm a surgeon,' he said, sounding miffed, and suddenly she found herself smiling.

And how could she not look? How could she not feel?

He was standing in the early-morning sun, dressed in the remnants of his dinner suit. His hair was rumpled; he obviously hadn't stopped to worry about personal grooming. He'd grabbed another branch and was about to heave.

'A surgeon,' she said, cautiously. 'So that makes you a chainsaw expert?'

'You're saying I'm not capable?'

'If you've been practising chainsawing on your patients for the last fifteen years, heaven help them.'

He grinned. It lit his face, making him look younger. It made him look like the Blake she remembered.

She felt her smile fade. Blake…

'Mardie, I'm sorry.' He wasn't coming close; there was half a ruined tree between them. 'I barge back into your life, I make stupid assumptions, I insult you, I try and land you with a blind dog…'

'Plus you didn't make the bacon crispy,' she retorted. 'I can forgive anything else.'

'I didn't…'

'Whatever you've been doing in the last fifteen years, it's not been cooking. Are those clothes very uncomfortable?'

'They're fine.' He paused, looked down at his sodden trousers, gave a rueful grimace. 'Okay, they're appalling.'

'I could lend you…'

'I don't want any more of your husband's clothes.'

'You didn't appreciate the bathrobe?'

'The bathrobe's excellent—although dry jocks would add a little something, even to the bathrobe.'

Dry jocks…

She blushed.

How long since she'd blushed? Her blushing used to kill her as a teenager. She thought she was over it.

She wasn't. She blushed. Over the mention of jocks. What, was she thirteen again?

'Hey,' Blake said, and suddenly his attention was no longer on her. Which was just as well. The blush was taking a while to subside. He stooped and peered at the slab of trunk that had peeled away. 'Look at this.'

She looked—and she blushed some more.

At ten years old, before she had any idea of vandalism, of desecration of trees, maybe before she had any sense at all, her dad had given her a pocket knife for her birthday. It had neat little tools on the side. It had her name engraved on the hilt. She'd loved that knife.

It hadn't always been a force for good—as displayed by what Blake was looking at.

The carving was at the base of the tree, practically in the dirt so only she knew it was there. It was cut into the bark and it had scored deeper and deeper as the tree grew.

M.R. xx B.M. A heart.

Blushing didn't begin to describe what was happening right now. She was about to go up in flames.

Blake was grinning.

'So I was dumb,' she snapped and reverted to chainsawing. Really loud. Loud was her salvation.

Would her blush never subside? She cut the lowest branch free, right through the middle of the initials.

M.R. xx…nobody. A heart all by itself.

He didn't comment.

They worked on, Mardie sawing, Blake carting timber.

Her blush and her head gradually cleared, and so did the driveway.

It would have taken her half a day to do this herself, but in an hour they had the driveway clear. The rest could be done over time. Not this morning, when she had Blake to get rid of.

She was so aware of him…

Stupid, stupid, stupid.

'Sheep?' he said, as she tossed the chainsaw onto the back of the tractor.

'Yep. I'll take the trailer off and head down and get them. I'll need Bounce.' She gave a man-sized whistle and Bounce came flying to her side.

Bessie emerged from the house. Reached the steps. Stopped.

'Can you stay with Bessie?' she asked, but Blake was already striding back to the house. Instead of going inside, though, he lifted Bessie down the steps, set her down and then headed back, Bessie at his side.

Mardie was removing the trailer from the tractor. Trying to block Blake out. She needed to head down the paddock and move the sheep—without a city doctor and a blind dog.

'It's rough going down there,' she said. 'I don't think...'

'Let her come,' he said gently. 'She's breaking her heart. She could sit at your feet on the tractor. There's room.'

'And when I get down there? I need to work. I can't...'

'I'll come with you.' Then, instead of waiting for her to agree, he climbed onto the running board, set Bessie at Mardie's feet and hung on himself. He looked down at Bounce, who was quivering all over, anticipating adventure. 'Sorry, mate, you're going to have to run behind.'

'He wouldn't have it any other way,' Mardie managed. And stupidly she felt like blushing again.

He was far too close. He was right...there. His shoulder was brushing her waist.

He expected her to calmly drive the tractor with him standing on the running board?

A woman could crash.

What were her hormones thinking?

Whatever they were thinking, they had nothing to do with her, she told herself. Her hormones could go take a cold shower. This guy was rude and insulting and an echo from her past she could do without.

It was just that he was so…close.

He'd ripped his shirt. He had a smear of mud down his face. He obviously had no shaving gear with him. His five-o'clock shadow was dark and…okay, and *sexy*.

She thought suddenly of her teenage James Bond fixation. Blake as James Bond at seventeen? Not even close.

Blake now…

He looked a lean, mean James Bond, she thought. And he was right by her side. She and James, off to face adventure with their two sleek adventure dogs.

Or off to move sheep with one silly pup and one blind stray.

'We should have brought the Lamborghini,' Blake said, and she glanced up at him in amazement.

They'd always had this. The ability to read what the other was thinking, to laugh even before the other was laughing.

She couldn't stop herself smiling.

'You want me to gun this baby?' she demanded. 'In fourth gear I reckon we can hit ten miles an hour. Three minutes tops from nought to ten. Who'd look for Formula One when we have my old tractor?'

He chuckled.

She loved his chuckle.

She loved Blake.

Huh?

No! She was old enough and sensible enough to stop herself right there. Once upon a time she'd loved Blake, with all the passion of her sixteen-year-old self, but even then she'd been sensible, knowing she couldn't follow him.

Now the sensible side of her kicked in again. She'd loved a seventeen-year-old Blake, but that wasn't who was standing on her running board. This guy must be what, thirty-two? He'd lived more of his life without her than with her. He had another life somewhere she knew nothing about.

He'd made all sorts of judgements about her, and she wasn't about to do the same to him.

She didn't know him any more.

'Are you married?' she asked suddenly. He was gazing out over the paddocks towards his aunt's old house, his eyes following the route they used to travel on their bikes, sometimes half a dozen times a day.

'Why do you want to know?'

'Because it's all been about me,' she said, exasperated. 'You've got my back-story, even down to the colour of bathrobe I hoped my husband liked. I know nothing.'

'You know I studied medicine.'

'And you know what I did. Snap. Now marriage. I've shown you mine, you show me yours.'

'Was yours happy?'

'Blake!'

He grinned at that, a trifle rueful. 'Yeah, I know. Unfair. It's just…' His voice trailed off.

'You did get married?'

'No,' he said. 'I was engaged for a bit. It didn't work out.'

'Oh, Blake…'

'Old history. I'm over it.'

'Another doctor?'

'Yes.'

'That makes sense.'

'What's that supposed to mean?'

'You wanted someone to share your life.' She hesitated. 'No. It was more than that. You needed someone to incorporate into your life. A marriage was never going to work on that basis.'

Silence. Her words had been mean, she thought. She should apologise. She did in her head but not out loud.

For some reason barriers were needed. She didn't need to get any closer to this man than she already was.

She needed him to get off the tractor. She needed him to stop touching her.

They reached the gate into the Cyprus paddock. 'Leave this one open,' she said.

He jumped down, and she was jolted by the sense of loss. How dumb was that?

He swung the gate wide, waited till she was through and then jumped up again. It was a prosaic action, done a score of times a day in her life, but she could tell... His face was revealing more than he could possibly know.

There were all sorts of sensations crowding in. The sensory experience of morning on a farm after rain... Something she almost took for granted but he'd lost fifteen years ago.

He hadn't lost it. He'd set it aside.

The Blake she knew was still in there.

The sheep were grazing near the Cyprus hedge. She'd used this paddock a few times recently and pickings were lean. The sheep headed towards the tractor as soon as they saw her coming, hopeful for hay.

'You're going to have to work for it,' she told them, turning thankfully to practical and prosaic. 'There's plenty of feed in the back paddocks, so you need to move.' She jumped down from the tractor—on the far side of Blake because there was no way she was brushing past him—and whistled to Bounce.

'Away to me,' she called. Firmly. Hopefully.

Eventually Bounce was going to be a brilliant working dog. He was desperate to please, and fiercely intelligent. Right now, however, he was just a bit too eager. Full of potential and hope.

He headed clockwise round the back of the pack as per order but he rushed, he went too close to the sheep and they startled. They started scattering before he could get to the back of the mob, spreading out in bleating sheep hysteria.

She'd have to run herself to get on the other side of them. She took off...

And suddenly Bessie was beside her, like a shadow, running in tandem, keeping pace.

The sheep reacted differently with the dogs. With her they were likely to run past, spread out, but Bessie's presence gave them pause. They fell back, uncertain. Bounce finally got round the back—and they started heading the way she wanted them to go, to the open paddock gate.

'Way back,' she yelled to Bounce and he streaked further back.

He barked.

And then Bessie was gone from her side, flying across the paddock to join Bounce at the rear, but on this flank.

She had two dogs at the back.

Bounce barked again and Bessie moved further back. She was well out of reach of the flock but they knew she was there.

How had she done that? *She was blind.*

There was no time to think about it now. Mardie sprinted towards the gate to stop them veering along the fence instead of through. But Blake was already there.

James Bond in his dinner suit, herding sheep.

The sheep crowded towards him, saw the open gate, hesitated.

Bessie barked.

Bounce crowded them behind.

James Bond held the gate.

They rushed through, a steady stream of non-panicked sheep, and the thing was done.

With just Bounce that might have taken her half an hour. They'd done it in minutes.

Blake swung the gate closed. 'How easy was that?' he demanded, grinning in satisfaction. 'Two good dogs...'

Both of them looked at Bessie.

As the sheep had flooded through the gate she'd paused, stopped. She'd have followed movement, light and sound. Now, things would simply be green again.

She sat, waiting for some sensory cue to move again.

Bounce headed to her side and sniffed. Rubbed himself against his new friend. Touched Bessie as she had touched him.

The start of a canine love affair?

Oh, for heaven's sake… She really was operating on hormones this morning. Mardie whistled. Bounce ran towards her and Bessie came with him.

Wagging her tail.

Wagging her whole body.

Border collies worked for pleasure. Herding sheep had been bred into them for generations.

This dog was seriously good.

She'd kept her distance from the flock. It was a bright morning and the sheep were washed clean with the rain. White against green…it had been possible for her to help.

And if she could help blind…

How much would it cost…?

'I'll pay,' Blake said and she blinked.

'Pardon?'

'I can't keep her,' he said. 'I know it's not fair to ask you to keep a dog I found, but you've always had more than one dog. I remember three.'

'I don't think…'

'She's born to work,' he said. 'She's almost as good blind as Bounce is now.'

'Bounce will get better,' she said, distracted and loyal. 'He's a work in progress.'

'And Bessie's a work of art. You know she's good. You could use her. I can afford…'

'It doesn't always work,' she said shortly. She'd thought this through it morning, with her face against Clarabelle's flank. It was the time she did her best thinking, but the conclusions she'd come to this morning were bleak. 'You think I'd do that to her? Send her to the city, two operations, each one risky. Weeks in a strange place, strange kennels, knowing

no one. She's done that already. She's been in the pound since
Charlie went into care. She's been thrown out of the Animal
Welfare van when it crashed and she's been wandering lost
for a week. You want me to put her through more trauma?'

'Yes,' he said bluntly. 'She could take it.'

'She can't.' Mardie squatted, clicking her fingers, and the
gentle little collie came to her. 'She's had enough, Blake,'
she said. 'To put her through operations with no guarantee
of success…'

But he wasn't accepting what she was saying. 'It would
succeed,' he said, just as firmly. He hesitated. 'Okay, there's
never a hundred per cent guarantee but it's close. She's a
young dog. These cataracts haven't been present for all that
long. I've had a good look. They're full, fluid-filled, not old
and shrinking. That means less risk of scarring. Underneath,
her eyes should be fine. There's a small risk of retina detachment with the operation, but with the best aftercare the risk
is tiny.'

'How do you know?'

'I do the same operation all the time on humans,' he said
simply. 'That's what I am, it's what I do—ophthalmology.
There's a vet in Sydney who spent time with me while we
were training. He's a personal friend and, Mardie, I know
he'll do this for me. I'll pay all the expenses and at the end of
it you'll have a fine working dog. I know she's my responsibility; I'm not asking you to take her on as a favour. I know
she'll be a fabulous dog. I know she can be cured.'

She stared up at him, stunned. 'But the cost…' She couldn't
think of anything more sensible to say.

'You know money's not an issue.'

Of course it wasn't. Somehow she forced herself not to look
at Blake, to look only at Bessie. To think only of Bessie. So
many things… To take this next step…

'I'd…I'd have to talk to Charlie,' she managed.

'Charlie?'

'The guy who owned her.'

'He put her in the pound.'

'He didn't have a choice. He was hospitalised himself.'

Bessie was being licked now by Bounce. Her week of escape had left her with interesting smells, and probably interesting tastes. Both dogs seemed deeply content.

Bessie and Bounce... Growing more devoted by the moment.

Hormones. Leave them out of this.

'How long would she need to stay in Sydney?' she asked, cautiously. Forcing herself to think past Blake. Beginning to think...maybe.

'Maybe a week. A few days before for tests and a few days after.'

'You'd be doing this because...'

'Call it thanks for the night's accommodation.'

'Then we'd be square again,' she said, a bit too harshly because suddenly...suddenly that was how she was feeling. Harsh. 'It wouldn't do to be in my debt.'

'Mardie...'

'I'm sorry, that's not very gracious.' She rose, reaching a decision. Regrouped. Tried very hard to put harsh behind her.

'Okay, so I don't want charity, but this is Bessie we're talking about. So that'd be it? You'd take her to Sydney, fix her eyes, give her back to me, no strings attached?'

'What do you mean—strings?'

'I'm not sure,' she said. 'It was only...that kiss. Blake, dumb or not, I don't want to go down the friendship path again. One cured dog, that's all this would be.'

'I never suggested anything else.'

She didn't reply.

She was being dumb.

He'd never suggested anything else. Of course he hadn't. So what...*else* was she thinking?

* * *

He hated not knowing what she was thinking. He'd always known.

He didn't know now.

He gazed around him, at the farm, at the sunlight on the wet grass, at the great crashed gum in the distance.

The shattered timber...

A friendship finished.

It wasn't about the kiss, he thought. It was about much more.

'I should have written,' he said softly into the morning stillness. 'I'm sorry I didn't. I was young and stupid and I didn't know how to handle my own grief at leaving.'

'You weren't sad to be going. You were jumping out of your skin.'

'I was,' he said. 'But I was sad to be leaving you. Gutted.'

'You didn't show it.'

'If I'd shown it,' he said simply, 'I never could have left.'

Then the outside world arrived. A police car pulled up out on the road, and Raff, the local cop, strolled across the paddocks to meet them. Someone had obviously reported Blake's crashed car.

'Hey,' Raff called. Blake knew Raff—he'd been part of the pack of local kids and he could see Raff recognised him in turn. Raff greeted him with warmth and a trace of relief. 'I heard you were at the reunion last night. When Gladys Mitchell called and said a Mercedes was wrapped round a tree I thought it must be you.' He grinned as he took in Blake's battered clothes. 'New fashion for farm work? Give the place a certain style, eh, Mardie? So what happened?'

He listened as a good cop should, but when he was told about Bessie his cheer slid away.

'Dogs,' he said bleakly. 'They're all over the place, and this one... At least Henrietta will be thankful she's found. You want me to take her back to town?'

'I'm keeping her,' Mardie said, and Raff looked from the dog to Mardie and back again.

'She's blind, Mardie,' he said, as if Mardie might not have noticed. 'I don't know how to say this but...'

'Blake says he'll fix her for me. He's an eye surgeon. He knows about cataracts. He'll take her back to Sydney and cure her.'

Raff whistled, stunned. 'You'd do that?'

'Yeah,' Blake said, feeling suddenly defensive. There was surprise in Raff's voice—amazement that an outsider was offering to help in what was essentially the town's business?

He'd never been part of this community, he thought. He'd been the rich kid. The kid who lived with the weird old lady. Now here he was, still on the outside, a guy in a dinner suit, offering charity.

But the charity, it seemed, was acceptable. 'Hen'll offer you her kingdom,' Raff said. 'Mind, her kingdom consists of lost dogs so I'd run a mile. But what about you, Mardie? Can you afford to keep another dog?'

Afford...

Were things so tight, then, that the cost of even keeping another dog would be a consideration?

'Of course I can. And she's good, Raff,' Mardie said. 'Great with sheep. I'll go in and talk to Charlie.'

'Charlie?'

'Her collar said she's Charlie's dog.'

Raff whistled at that, too. 'Of course. I remember... She'll be great, then. Charlie's been amazing,' he told Blake. 'In his day he's been the best dog-trainer in the district. Took every championship going.'

And Blake suddenly remembered.

Just before Mardie's dad died he'd taken them to the local sheepdog trials. They'd seen an elderly man in a battered coat and wide-brimmed hat take all the awards going. Charlie. Charlie's dogs had moved sheep so skilfully they might as well be attached to them by leads. The dogs simply looked at the sheep and the sheep jumped to obey.

'I'll learn how to do that,' Mardie had declared, and he couldn't help himself—he looked at Bounce. Who was still sort of…bouncing.

'He's a work in progress,' Mardie repeated defensively, and he grinned.

'I can see that. Taking a while to settle.'

'Bessie'll teach him,' she said. 'When she's better.'

'So you are serious?' Raff asked Blake. 'Will you take her to Sydney with you now?'

And Blake got that, too. This guy was interested in practicalities and he was also protecting his own. He wasn't having Mardie landed with a blind dog and a half-promise to fix her. Maybe Raff knew, as Blake did, that once Mardie took Bessie on, she'd keep her, regardless.

Once Mardie gave her heart, she didn't take it back.

And that was a kick in the guts, too.

She'd married?

What was she supposed to have done? Had he expected her to stay loyal to him for fifteen years? Pining for a memory?

He'd moved on. So had she.

'I need to contact my vet friend,' he said, but he was speaking to Mardie. He was thinking of Mardie, feeling bad. Okay, he'd let her down in the past, but on this at least he could make good. 'I don't know when he could fit her in. And I'll need to get her there. I imagine I'll need to take the bus back to Sydney and come back once I've organised a car.'

'I'll take you back to Sydney,' Mardie said.

Silence.

Mardie, driving him back to Sydney.

It was little more than a two-hour drive.

Why not?

It was just that…

He saw the corners of her mouth twitch. Uh-oh. She'd guessed his errant thought. His dumb thought.

'I'm guessing Blake's worrying that Sydney's a big, big city and I might rightfully be scared,' she told Raff, her eyes suddenly alight with laughter. 'But I hear there's folk who've visited and come out alive.' She snagged a blade of grass and started chewing. Country hick personified. 'Ain't that right, Raff?'

'He's right in that there's perils aplenty,' Raff said gravely, cop-like, catching on in an instant.

'Like what?' she said and put on an anxious face.

'Restrooms,' Raff drawled back. 'Fearsome places. They teach us in cop school. If you use a city restroom, don't sit on the seat—city germs'll kill you before you can put your shopping on the floor. And don't put your feet on the ground or you'll be hit by a syringe from under the stalls. White slave traders,' he said, his voice loaded with doom. 'You'll wake up in a harem in Bathsheba. You reckon you can risk that, our Mardie?'

Mardie grinned. At Raff, not at him.

'I reckon I'll take my chances. Lorraine'll look after my place for a while. Mum's happy right now. The forecast for the weather's settled. It'll do me good to have a few days away.'

Whoa, Blake thought. A few days? She was coming to Sydney as in...*coming to stay*?

'My aunt's apartment only has one bedroom,' he said before he could stop himself.

Mardie's grin widened. She and Raff were still enjoying their joke. 'Not a harem, then?'

'Um...' He managed a limp smile. 'No.'

'Too bad. But I have somewhere I can stay in Sydney,' she said quite kindly. 'In Coogee. I can take Bounce there. It'll be easier on Bessie if Bounce is close; a semblance of normality. Is Coogee close to where Bessie will need to be looked after?'

'Yes.' As luck would have it, the next suburb to Central Vets.

But… How come she had a place to stay in Sydney? The way she and Raff were laughing…she went often?

There were a million questions he wanted to ask.

He was an outsider. He had no right to ask.

'I'll catch the bus back to Sydney,' he said, not knowing what else to say. 'I'll let you know about Bessie's operation and you can come as soon as it's scheduled.'

'Organise it now,' Raff said, laughter giving way to cop in charge.

'You don't trust me?'

'I don't want Mardie landed with a blind dog.' Raff's smile died. 'You haven't been near the place for fifteen years. Why should I trust you? Sorry, mate, but my job's looking out for this community.'

'I keep my word.'

'I trust him,' Mardie said.

It needed only that—that she gave him a reference as well as everything else. But he glanced at her and she met his gaze and he saw…

It was more than words. She was meeting his gaze head-on, her eyes clear and steady, and he knew that a decision had been taken.

He'd lost something fifteen years ago. A tiny part of that was being given back.

He smiled at her, and she smiled straight back, a wide, cheeky smile that was almost daring.

He'd forgotten how lovely that smile was.

Or maybe he'd always remembered but he'd locked it away in a corner that had stayed locked; a corner that held things that hurt too much to take out and examine.

A corner that held Robbie?

'You have a change of clothes somewhere?' Raff asked, watching them both with a bemused expression. It was a cop expression, giving nothing away but maybe understanding more than they wanted.

'No, I…'

'There's nothing in the car except your laptop and brief-case,' Raff said. 'I searched it. I also wasted a few minutes searching in case you were dead. You might have phoned, Mardie.'

'The phone's down.'

He swore. 'Sorry, that's right, a tree crashed on the lines between town and here. It should be up by lunchtime. Okay, moving on, you need to organise the dog and then you need to organise something to wear. You go out in public like that and I'll have calls to arrest you for indecent exposure.'

Raff was right. He was indecent. His ripped shirt was hardly there.

Both Mardie and Raff were gazing at him. Raff with spec-ulation. Mardie with…something else.

She started to smile and then…suddenly her smile turned again into a blush. He watched as she fought, but failed, to keep her colour under control.

It wasn't just a blush. It was sheer, breathtaking beauty. Mardie…

'I'll take him into town and buy some gear,' she managed, trying to sound practical despite the blush. 'If he can orga-nise Bessie's operation for this week I'll take them both to Sydney tomorrow.'

'Excuse me,' he said. 'Is this about me? And I can take the bus.'

'Don't look a gift horse in the mouth,' Raff said shortly. 'If Mardie's happy to take you… Sunday's the soccer bus. You don't know what you're missing.'

'I can't stay here another night.'

'There are bed and breakfasts in town,' Raff said. 'Though most of your reunion lot are staying for the weekend. You'll be lucky to find anywhere.'

'Don't be dumb,' Mardie said. 'You can stay and help me get rid of the rest of the tree.'

'Organise the vet first,' Raff said.

'I told you, Raff, I trust him.'

'Yeah, you'd trust anyone,' Raff said and handed Blake his radio. 'Satellite,' he said. 'I can get signal anywhere. For emergency cop stuff. Or, in this instance, emergency dog stuff and protecting-Mardie duty. If Mardie's putting you up for the weekend and you're imposing a dog on her, it's the least I can do. Mardie might trust you. I want proof. Ring your mate and see if you can get this operation organised. Now.'

CHAPTER FIVE

COLIN could do it. 'For no one else,' he said, 'but for you, yes. I leave gaps for emergencies. Cataracts don't usually rate but in this case I'll slot her in. I'll need her here three days beforehand for tests and eye-drops. If everything's good then I'll schedule surgery for Thursday. She'll need careful monitoring afterwards but you should be able to do that yourself.'

He'd worry about aftercare later, Blake decided, relaying the part about surgery and tests but not the aftercare. He knew it'd be complicated, and things were complicated enough.

Raff left, promising to send a tow truck for the car. Promising to let Henrietta know about Bessie.

He left grinning.

He'd backed Blake into a corner. Instant dog surgery.

He'd backed him into staying another night with Mardie.

Staying with Mardie was the biggie. He felt… It felt…

As if he was out of control, and Blake Maddock was a man who didn't like being out of control.

The trip into town made him feel even worse. Mardie had offered to buy clothes for him, but that seemed weird. What he hadn't thought through was how weird it would be to walk into Morrisy Drapers and have every person in the shop recognise him.

They already knew what had happened. Of course. Banksia Bay was like that. He was wearing his battered dinner-suit trousers and Raff's spare jacket with cop insignia. Inconspicuous R Us.

He felt like a flashing neon.

'Oh, you poor boy.' Mrs Connor, who ran Morrisy Drapers, was a gusher. 'We hear your car's a write-off. But Raff says it's a rental car so that's lucky. But you were even luckier you weren't killed. And all for a stray dog. My old dad says never swerve for animals. They're not worth losing your life over.'

'Bessie's lucky he did,' Mardie said roundly. 'How could he not try to miss her? And he didn't risk his life. He was driving a tank.'

'A Mercedes isn't a tank,' Mrs Connor said, shocked, as she handed clothes over the counter. 'A tank's what you drive.'

'My truck's not a tank. It's practically luxury,' Mardie retorted. 'Isn't that right, Blake?'

Blake glanced outside to where they'd parked the truck. It was an ancient Dodge, built, he suspected, to withstand the Huns.

Definitely tankish. Though most tanks didn't have rust.

'Um…pure driving pleasure,' he managed and he was rewarded by Mardie's smile. It was a truly gorgeous smile.

It always had been a gorgeous smile. He hadn't realised how much he'd missed it.

'It's definitely classy,' Mardie declared, eyeing Blake's pile of sensible clothes with approval. 'Like these. Jeans and T-shirt, pure class. What about boots, Mrs Connor?'

'Work boots or nothing,' Mrs Connor said.

'Excellent,' Mardie decreed. 'We have twenty-four hours before we head to Sydney and I intend to put him to work. You want to change here, Blake, before we head to the nursing home?'

'We're going to the nursing home?' He wanted to go straight back to Mardie's. Actually, he wanted to go straight back to Sydney but it wasn't happening. It was Mardie who was giving orders. He was on her turf, doing what she wanted.

The nursing home it was. Her mother, Etta.

'I need to see Mum,' she said. 'I need to organise a few days away, and we also need to see Charlie, to explain that you found his dog and you're going to save her. Mum will love to see you.'

'It might be better if you go alone,' he said diffidently, and she looked at him as if he was crazy.

'Better for who?'

'For your mum.' Etta had been so good to him. He should have kept in touch. Why make her remember what a stupid kid he'd been? 'I've been no part of your mother's life for a long time now,' he said, almost to himself. 'It's best to leave things as they are.'

She looked at him for a long, considering minute. Looked as if she was about to say something and then thought better of it. Reconsidered.

'Fine,' she said at last. 'Stay in the truck. Stay nice and uninvolved, like you have for fifteen years.'

Mardie checked in at the nurses' station first. She worked here three days a week. She needed to organise time away.

Liz, the nurse administrator, greeted her with unconcealed curiosity. She was practically vibrating with her need to know. 'So the rumours are true. Blake Maddock's back.'

'I hate this town.'

Liz giggled. 'We're fast. I hear he's hot. You guys were such an item…'

'Fifteen years ago,' she retorted. 'Will you cut it out?'

'You're not the least bit interested?'

'No!' That was a lie, but the guy was sitting out in the truck being uninvolved. It'd pay her to be uninvolved as well. Very uninvolved.

'Yet you're going to Sydney with him.'

'I really hate this town. Yes, but I'm not staying anywhere

near him. I'll stay at Irena's. He's organising the operation on Bessie's eyes, that's all.'

Liz's smile faded. 'Bessie. Raff told Henrietta you found Charlie's dog. You really think the operation will work?'

'Blake's an eye surgeon. He says it will.'

'It'll be the best gift you could give to Charlie. Did you bring her with you?'

'I wasn't sure if I should.' She hesitated. 'Would it be kind?'

Liz considered and then grimaced. 'Maybe not. He gave her to the pound, and it nearly killed him. If the operation doesn't work... For him to say goodbye again...'

'You think I shouldn't tell him we're trying?'

'He already knows she's been found. This is Banksia Bay, after all. Tell him what's happening, but it might stress him too much to see her. Operations sometimes fail, regardless of what your Blake says.'

'He's not my Blake!'

'Regardless of what *anyone's* Blake says,' Liz retorted, her smile returning. 'Get her better and bring her in then. Meanwhile, don't worry about your mum; you know we'll look after her. And even though we love your craft classes, we all know how long it's been since you've had a break. Take a real holiday. Have some fun. If anyone deserves it, you do.'

And then she paused. Someone was strolling past her window.

Her eyes widened. 'Oh, my...'

Mardie followed her gaze.

Blake.

Jeans. T-shirt. Work boots.

Body to die for.

'Oh, my,' Liz repeated, mocking fanning herself. 'If I'd known he was going to turn out like this I would have snagged him in grade school. Only, of course, you got in first.'

'I did not!'

'You did, too.'

'Yeah, well, if I did it's all in the past,' Mardie said hotly. 'He wiped Banksia Bay from the map when he left.'

'Yeah, but a woman could forgive a lot of a guy who looks like this.'

'Not this woman,' Mardie retorted. 'I have a long memory.'

'Boyfriend-girlfriend fights from fifteen years ago?' Liz chuckled. 'With that package in front of me I'd get over it fast. People change.' But then Liz held up her hands as if in surrender. 'Okay, sweetie, if anger's needed to keep you safe, then stick to your anger. But don't let it mess with fun. Say goodbye to your mum and then go to Sydney—and you keep an open mind.'

Then she glanced again at Blake and fanned herself some more.

'A very open mind,' she repeated. 'A girl'd be a fool not to.'

Mardie's mother was playing solitaire. She glanced up as Blake opened the door and her eyes grew huge. She recognised him in an instant.

'Blake Maddock. Oh, my boy…' Somehow she pushed herself stiffly to wobbly feet and held out her arms.

It took a moment to respond. He stood in the doorway, looking at the woman who'd been practically a mother to him. She'd been far more a mother than his own.

She'd been burdened with arthritis for all the time he remembered, but he'd never seen anything but cheer. She'd lived surrounded by chaos, the radio always on, her kitchen table always laden with her next creation. Her cooking trials had been truly scary. He and Mardie would appear for lunch, Mardie's dad would be looking terrified and Etta would be saying firmly, 'You can eat it or not, there's always eggs on toast, but give it three bites first.'

Chocolate pudding with chilli. Duck à l'orange, only: 'We can't afford duck so I shaped a duck with mince instead. Do you think it looks like a duck?'

Crazy stuff.

Wonderful. Fun.

He'd loved it.

He'd loved Etta. And Bill.

And Mardie.

He should have stayed in touch. He'd been a stupid kid, he'd long accepted his reasons for leaving, but still he felt bad.

Regardless, here was Etta, wobbly on her feet, standing with open arms. Tears were slipping down her cheeks and she was smiling and smiling. 'Blake,' she said again and he walked forward and hugged her.

Mardie walked in the door and her mother was hugging Blake. No, her mother was being hugged. She'd been lifted right off her feet, and she was crying, laughing and railing against him, all at once. 'Put me down, you silly boy. You'll do yourself a damage. Ooh, put me down.'

Blake and her mother…

She stopped short in the doorway and she felt as if the earth had shifted.

Her mother adored Blake. From the time he'd first been allowed past the boundaries of his great-aunt's property, Etta had welcomed him with open arms.

'You ring your aunt and ask if you can stay for lunch,' she'd say, and Blake would look at the crazy experiment on the kitchen table and jump right in.

'Yes, please. That looks…really yummy, Mrs Rainey.'

Now… It was as if she was welcoming home a long-lost son. But Mardie had watched her mother wait for news from Blake, as she herself had waited. She wasn't feeling so welcoming.

If she let herself be as welcoming as her mum… Dangerous territory. She felt as if she were teetering on the edge of some kind of abyss and she needed to step back fast.

She needed to be happy. Bouncy. Impersonal. She pinned

on a smile and forced her voice to brightness. 'Isn't it great he's here? Did he tell you he crashed his car last night?'

'No!' Her mother sank back into her armchair, looking at Blake with such an expression...

How could Blake walk away and come back and still be loved? Mardie thought.

He hadn't expected it. He didn't want it. She could read Blake's face and she could see regret and dismay.

He didn't show it in his voice. Instead, he told Etta about the crash, making it funny. He told her about Bessie, making the story sad but hopeful. By the end Etta was demanding they bring her in.

'We can't,' Blake said and told her about Charlie.

'Oh, of course. So you'll fix her and bring her back to visit him all better?' Etta's eyes were shining.

'We'll fix her and then Mardie can bring her in.'

'You come in,' Etta said, suddenly stern. 'I bet Charlie remembers you. He'd love that.'

'My life's in Sydney. And overseas.'

'People only go overseas for visits, and Sydney's a two-hours drive away. If you can go overseas you can come here.'

'Bessie will be Mardie's dog,' he said, gently but inexorably. 'I don't have a place here any more.'

'There's a place in Mardie's spare room, any time you want,' Etta said with asperity. 'That's fine with you, Mardie, isn't it?'

Maybe not. But Mardie didn't say so. She gave her mother a reassuring smile, she said of course Blake could always stay, and she knew that Blake intended nothing of the kind.

He'd walked away. He was home by accident, but it wasn't his home.

He couldn't wait to get away from Banksia Bay. Nothing had changed.

* * *

They left Etta, and walked silently to Charlie's room.

Blake was feeling disoriented, as if shadows of the past were reaching out to touch him. Mardie was silent by his side.

She'd been angry with him—she was angry with him. He'd forgiven himself, he thought. He'd figured why his teenage self had acted as he had. Justifying it to Mardie seemed harder.

Justifying it wasn't necessary. He didn't need to tell Mardie…

Maybe he did. Maybe that was the whole reason he'd come home.

Not home. Banksia Bay.

Regardless, now wasn't the time.

Charlie Hunter had once been a big man. No longer. He'd shrivelled with age, and his last stroke had left him paralysed down his left side. He lay motionless, surrounded by memorabilia. Trophies and ribbons. Photographs of dogs. A gorgeous enamelled plate showing Charlie—with dogs. Leads, collars, framed Australian Championship certificates. A lifetime of dogs.

'My Bessie,' he whispered as Blake told him what had happened, what they hoped to do. He could barely get the words out.

'If you don't want…'

But where there'd been apathy and defeat, suddenly there was fire. 'Are you dreaming?' he demanded. 'If I'd had the money, her eyes would have been fixed two years back.' Charlie's words were distorted with paralysis, but he said them loud and strong so they couldn't be mistaken. 'But these last two years, since my first stroke…well, a blind dog wasn't what I needed. It wasn't fair on her, though. She spent her life at my feet, never whining, just there for me. But when she was a pup…the joy of her…'

He paused and fought for breath. Fought for strength to go on. 'It would have been kinder to put her down,' he whispered. I just…couldn't. So finally I sent her to the pound in-stead. What a cop-out. If you could cure her…'

'No promises,' Blake told him. 'But we'll try.'

'You're a good lad,' Charlie whispered. 'I remember my Hilda talking about you, saying she had no idea how such a miserable old grouch as your aunt deserved a kid with such a good heart. And happy. You were happy as a kid.'

Happy. There was that word again. It caught Blake like a faltering of the heart.

Happy was for childhood. Not for now. Now was for keep-ing promises.

Without going back to Africa?

It wasn't the time to think of that now. Get out of Banksia Bay and then think it through.

'Bessie'll be back here soon,' he told Charlie. He was sounding too brusque but there was nothing he could do about it. 'Mardie will bring her in as soon as she gets back from Sydney.'

'That's a promise,' Mardie said and he caught another edge of anger. Fair enough. He was promising Mardie's time. He was promising Mardie would see things through.

She would, though. She was the dependable one.

She was the one who stayed at home while he moved on.

Mardie had things to do for the rest of the day. It seemed leaving the farm for over a week involved organisation and she didn't want his help.

'Find a book and give your head a rest,' she told him. 'Lie by the fire and think how lucky you were last night.'

She headed out to see someone called Lorraine, who'd look after the place while she was absent.

He was left with the dogs.

He *was* tired.

He picked up a copy of the *Farmers Weekly* and tried to read.

The dogs lay in front of the fire and tried to settle.

They were all doleful.

Enough. Yes, his head was aching; yes, there were bruises which hurt; the aches from dengue were still with him but lying around made him think of them more.

He had proper clothes now. He could do proper stuff.

He put on his boots and both dogs were alert and at the door in an instant. Together they had it figured; Bounce maintained contact with Bessie as if he realised how much she needed him.

Smartest dogs in the world. Bonding with each other while he watched.

It'd be a joy to give Bessie back her sight, he thought, a joy for Bounce as well as for Bessie.

It'd also be a joy for Mardie. A gift he could leave her with.

The thought was a good one. He headed outside, a dog at each heel, feeling better.

He intended to go for a walk over the farm. He did for a bit. Things looked the same. There was a new shed out the back, seriously big, that had him intrigued, but it was locked.

Was this a guy's shed, he wondered, locked after Hugh died? The thought of Hugh left him feeling strangely empty. Sad that he hadn't kept in touch. That he hadn't been here for her. That there was a part of Mardie he didn't know?

He didn't want to walk any further, he decided. He didn't want to end up at his aunt's crazy mansion which, according to the guys he'd talked to at the reunion, was now boarded up, after the spa operators who'd bought it had gone bankrupt.

Despite the hour, he was tired. Dengue had left him with residual fatigue that was taking months to recede.

But to sleep seemed impossible. Instead, he headed for the massive pile of ruined tree.

They'd cleared a path down the driveway, but heaped on either side were mounds of splintered timber yet to be moved.

How long since he'd played with a chainsaw?

This was a man's job. Fatigue receded in the face of a plan. He grinned and practically felt his chest expand. 'We can do this,' he told the dogs and he felt their quiver of excitement, responding to his enthusiasm. Man with chainsaw.

'So chainsaw, tractor, trailer. I hope she's left the keys. Let's see how much we can get done before she gets back.' It was a small enough token of his thanks, he thought.

Chainsaw. Excellent.

He found the chainsaw in the unlocked shed by the house. On close inspection it seemed a truly excellent power tool. He'd been frankly jealous of Mardie wielding it this morning. 'Nothing to this,' he told the dogs, who both gave rather dubious wags of their tails.

'Okay, you guys can stand back,' he told them. 'You count the logs as I stack 'em for firewood.'

Bounce looked at Bessie and whined. She moved in close and both dogs headed off to the bottom paddock.

Getting some exercise, or abandoning the *Titanic*?

'Dumb dogs,' Blake said. He heaved his chainsaw across his shoulder and headed for the tree.

She hadn't meant to be away for so long, but Lorraine was aching to show her a vase she'd created and to demonstrate a technique she felt could take her in another direction.

Lorraine was a potter. Mardie was an enameller. Together they'd just invested everything they owned and a bit more into a state-of-the-art kiln—a kiln to die for. They could both do so much now they had it.

Lorraine's enthusiasm was infectious, and at home was… Blake. It was worth talking enamelling, talking potting, so she didn't have to go home to Blake. Blake, whose mere presence had her discombobulated.

But she couldn't stay away for ever. Finally she said goodbye to Lorraine. She headed home.

She turned into the drive and slowed.

They'd cleared the driveway this morning, but there'd been a mass of timber left on either side.

Blake must have worked like a man possessed. The pile of logs beside the woodshed was four times what it had been this morning.

And the remains of the trunk… She was close enough to see. Close enough to…

No!

For what was left of the trunk, still standing tall this morning, had now crashed to the side of the driveway.

And worse…

Behind the massive trunk she could see…Blake on the tractor, slumped over the wheel. Unconscious?

She was out of the truck before she knew it, screaming without words. Or maybe there were words, just the one.

No. No. No.

Running.

'Blake…'

She was clambering across fallen branches, stumbling, ripping branches aside. Feeling cold, empty terror. 'Blake!'

She thought…she thought…

'Blake!'

He lifted his head from the steering wheel. Pushed himself up. Spoke.

'Mardie?'

Alive…

Her heart kick-started again. Just.

Blake. Alive.

He sounded dazed. Half asleep? 'I got it down,' he said. 'The whole thing.'

There was even a tinge of pride in his voice.

He got it down.

Terror receded, leaving a void where things didn't make sense. She was struggling to take it in.

She was in the middle of a crush of timber.

Blake was alive.

'I thought you were dead,' she said stupidly, not believing what she was seeing. 'I thought…'

'I went to sleep,' he said apologetically. 'I cleared the branches that fell, and then I thought I could get the rest of the trunk down. It took more than I thought.'

Asleep.

'I thought…' she said and then stopped.

He'd seen her face now. She knew she wouldn't have a vestige of colour left.

'I had dengue fever,' he said apologetically. 'It takes it out of me. I really wanted to get it down. Then I brought the tractor and trailer close to clear the mess but I thought…' He gave her an apologetic smile. 'The sun felt great. I thought I'd take a quick nana nap.'

A nana nap. He'd been taking a nana nap while she thought he'd been brained by a tree.

She gazed around her, taking great gulps of air. Maybe she'd forgotten to breathe.

He'd cleared half a tree.

Then he'd had a nana nap.

'I might have been slightly ambitious,' he conceded. 'I had this idea of clearing the lot before you got home, and it's a great chainsaw.'

'It…it is,' she agreed. Paused. Took a few more breaths. Then had to say it out loud. The thing that was hammering in her head. 'You could have been killed. I thought you had been.'

She started to shake.

She couldn't stop.

She couldn't…

And suddenly he was stomping across the pile of crushed wood and leaf litter until he reached her.

He held her shoulders and he held her tight.

'Mardie, it's okay. Nothing's hurt. I knew what I was doing.

The tractor and I were on the other side of the driveway when it came down. It only looks bad because I brought the trailer in close to start clearing up.'

She couldn't hear. His words were a buzz.

The events of the past, surging back. Moments that had transformed her life.

Her father, folding as he walked in from out in the paddocks. Dead in an instant.

Hugh. One stupid moment, stupid kids in a too-fast car, and his life was over.

And again… The instant she'd seen the fallen tree and Blake slumped over the wheel.

Reaction took over, leaving her no choice in how she responded. She tried to shove back from his hold and she yelled, as she'd never yelled in her life.

'You stupid, stupid moron. You used a chainsaw when no one was home. Don't you realise the first rule, *the first rule*, is to have someone with you when you use big power tools? You just chopped. Macho, macho stupidity. You've given me half a winter's full of chopped wood and what good would that have done if you were dead?'

'You'd have been warm,' he said cautiously. Still holding her.

She wasn't responding to humour. She couldn't. 'It's cold in the cemetery.' She was still yelling.

'Yes, but it's me who'd have been there, not you. But it didn't happen. Mardie, it didn't happen. It was never going to happen. Believe it or not, I knew what I was doing. I'm sorry I didn't finish clearing it. I wanted to. I'll pay to…'

'*Pay?* I don't care about payment.' She was still hysterical. 'I'm not in this for money. I'm not the one who walked away to make money.'

And suddenly it was about more than the tractor. More than this moment. Much more. She was out of control and she was saying it like it was. Years of hurt, welled up and finally released.

'I walked away to make money?' he said cautiously.

'You never looked back,' she said, still out of control. 'Not once. You and your aunt and your stupid, rich family who couldn't even look after a kid, and your stupid money making. If you'd been killed now it'd be no less than you deserve. Of all the stupid things…' She caught her breath on an angry sob. 'I could have lost you again. And now you've brought down the rest of the tree and we'll have to clear this and all you can think of is paying.'

She'd almost lost him again.

She heard her words echo, reverberate. They'd come straight from her heart.

They both knew it.

She was shaking as if she'd stepped out of an ice box. Her teeth were chattering so hard she could hardly get the words out.

There were tears tracking down her face. The night Hugh died… The day her father collapsed…

The day Blake left.

The dogs moved close to the base of the mess of tree and whined, worried by her yelling. *She* was worried by her yelling. She didn't get out of control.

She was out of control now.

She was still in the middle of the leaf litter. Blake was still holding her.

The branch under them sagged.

And suddenly Blake was in charge. He took her by the waist and lifted her free, tugging her down to solid ground. He set her in front of him but didn't release her.

He held her round the waist as she trembled. Holding her tight. Not saying a thing. She tugged away, but not very hard. Not enough to succeed.

'What…what do you think you're doing?' she managed.

'Waiting until you get over the shock. Trying to reassure you that it's okay.'

'It isn't.'

'Tell me what happened, Mardie,' he said softly. 'The car crash. Was that how your husband died?'

'I… Yes.' There was nothing else to say.

'Here?'

She didn't want to tell him. She never talked about it.

She told him.

'We were driving home from Lorraine's, up the road. A Christmas barbecue.' Her voice was still shaking. Her world was still shaking. 'Six o'clock on a warm Sunday night. A carload of kids came round a blind bend on the wrong side of the road and that was…that. I ended up with a fractured pelvis. But Hugh…my gentle, loving Hugh who'd give me the world, who gave me the world, was gone in an instant. And the dogs. All our dogs. They were in the back.' Another sob. The urge to yell was back, but she couldn't raise the energy. She felt desperately tired. 'And you…you play with chainsaws as if it doesn't matter one bit. You just…risk…'

It was too much. She choked on a sob, her knees gave way from under her and he drew her into him.

For a fraction of a moment she resisted, holding herself rigid. He could feel her anger. He could feel her fear.

But he could feel her shaking and it was the shaking that killed her resistance. She crumpled and he gathered her against him and held and held, as if there was nothing more important than to hold her against his heart and let the world go on without them.

Nothing was more important.

The dogs stood beside them, silent sentinels. Neither moved, as if both realised this moment couldn't be interrupted by a wet nose; it couldn't be interrupted for the world.

He simply held her.

Had she had someone to hold her when Hugh died? he wondered. Two years ago.

Had Mardie buried her husband and come home to an empty house?

The dogs…

He thought of them now. Minor in the scheme of things, minor compared to a husband, but still…

Every time he'd been to this place there'd been a dog pack. 'You need generations of dogs, training each other.' He remembered Mardie's father saying it. 'You lose a dog, it's a heartbreak. You lose all your dogs…' He'd shrugged. 'I don't know how a man could go on without them.'

Bounce was Mardie's only dog, and he was only about twelve months old. That meant it must have been twelve months before she could even bear to get another dog.

He'd have been in Africa. He scanned Australian news on the internet, but never in such detail as names of car crash victims. If he'd known…

The shaking was starting to subside. She tugged away a little and he released her to arm's length, no further.

'Tell me about Hugh,' he said softly, and she managed a ghost of a smile. Realising he was trying to haul her from shock. Trying to respond.

'He was from Whale Cove. Practically a foreigner.'

He smiled, straight into her eyes. It was a smile he couldn't remember using before. Or maybe he had. It was a smile just for Mardie.

'You met him at Whale Cove?'

'That's where I did my art course. He was a paramedic, an ambulance driver. He was gentle, kind, loving…all I ever wanted in a husband. We were friends for ages, were engaged for two years, married for three.'

'He lived with you here?'

'There was Mum.' She was recovering a little but her voice was still shaky. 'We couldn't leave her, and Hugh was happy to transfer to Banksia Bay. Then, when she finally decided to move to the nursing home, Hugh said he loved this place as much as I did. It would have been a great place for our children...' She broke off. Closed her eyes.

'Enough,' she said. 'We have stuff to organise.' She stared at the driveway. 'This to clear, for a start.'

'No.'

'No?'

'I think,' he said apologetically, 'that neither of us should use the chainsaw for a while.'

'You want me to come home to this mess?'

'I've fixed that.'

'It doesn't look fixed.' Indignation was returning. Indignation versus shaking? He almost smiled. Indignation any day.

'That's what I was talking of when I mentioned paying,' he said. Whether or not the shaking had stopped, he was still holding her and she was still allowing herself to be held. 'I rang Raff. He gave me the name of a guy who chops wood for a living. Tony Kennedy'll be here at eight on Monday to clear the mess.'

'But you're already covering the cost of Bessie's operation,' she managed, sounding stunned.

'You know I can afford it.'

There was a moment's silence at that, drawn out, tense, loaded with something he didn't recognise.

'I don't...take charity,' she said at last.

'I don't believe I'm offering charity. I'm responsible.'

'You're not responsible for Bessie.'

'I'm not paying for Bessie for you. I'm paying for Bessie for me. But, regardless, I owe you.'

'Why do you owe me?' she asked in a strange, tight voice.

That, at least, was easy.

'You and your parents made my childhood bearable,' he

said simply and firmly. 'I owe you a debt I can never repay. I should have been here for you two years ago. That I wasn't…'

He let the sentence hang.

Silence. More silence. He wasn't sure what to say next. How to begin to make things better?

There was no way.

Mardie was watching him. Her face was calm. Assessing.

Very calm. And suddenly he thought…it was like the eye of the storm.

He could almost feel the other side.

'Do you think I needed you?' she asked, almost diffident.

'I assume…'

'Assume nothing.'

'Sorry?'

'Do you think I spent the last fifteen years pining for you?' she asked, still in that strangely calm voice.

'I know that's not true.'

'You do,' she said cordially. 'Yes, at sixteen you were my boyfriend. I wept for weeks when you left. But weeks, Blake Maddock, not years. And then you know what? I got angry. And then I got over it.'

'Good for you.'

'Don't patronise me,' she snapped, and the storm moved closer. With the potential to build. 'Of all the…'

'I didn't mean to patronise.'

'Yes, you did,' she said. 'You do. You're sorry you weren't here for me two years ago. As if somehow, magically, you could have made it better.'

'I never meant that.'

'Good,' she said. 'I'm glad you didn't mean it. Because it wouldn't have made one whit of difference. Do you know how surrounded I was?'

'No, I…'

'I was loved,' she said. 'I *am* loved. Don't you dare think of me as poor, lonely Mardie, facing the big bad world because heroic Blake Maddock wasn't here to take care of her. This place is my home. I'm loved. When people are in trouble here, we help. I had a broken pelvis and my husband was dead but I had my community to surround me. My freezer still contains so many home-cooked meals that I could live on tuna bakes for years. My sheep were cared for, my fences fixed, my house painted. My garden was replanted so that I've had veggies and flowers ever since. I have a friend who came and stayed for two months—Irena. I was cosseted to bits. And here you are saying you're so sorry you weren't here for me, as if it would have made a blind bit of difference.'

She took a deep breath, the calm façade cracking wide open. 'And you know what? It's great that you've organised this tree to be cleared, and I accept with pleasure. But I don't depend on it. If I'm in trouble, I have a town full of people who'll help. If I rang up a few friends and said I can't cope with a fallen tree I'd have a working bee here in minutes. You know…'

Another breath.

'Last winter I got the flu. I didn't let anyone know because I hate fuss, only then I ran out of wood. The place was cold, and I was too tired to get out of bed and chop some. Then Liz arrived. She's the administrator of Mum's nursing home. I'd rung and said I had a cold and couldn't come in, but Liz thought she'd check anyway. She practically called out the army. An hour later the house was a furnace, there was food, fuss, heat packs, every home remedy known to man. I was so coddled I had no choice but to get better.'

'That's…great.' It was a pathetic comment but what else was he to say?

But she hadn't stopped. She'd barely paused for breath.

'And you know what?' she snapped. 'It all happened without you. And now… I love it that you're helping with Bessie. I'm grateful you've organised the tree. But don't you dare think I'll fall in a heap without you. I spent a few weeks in tears as a lovesick teenager and then I moved on. Now, if you don't mind, I have things to do to get my life in order before I leave. And, believe it or not, I can do all those things by myself.'

CHAPTER SIX

THE power came on.

Mardie headed down the paddocks to do one last run around the sheep before dinner.

He suspected she didn't need to. He suspected she didn't want to be in the house with him.

The tow-truck driver arrived and shook his head over the Mercedes. Blake had already rung the hire-car firm; insurance would sort it from here. He retrieved his laptop and briefcase, watched the wrecked Mercedes be towed away, and then went back to the house and set up his laptop in the attic.

It might be wise to lie low for a while, he thought. Leave Mardie to settle down.

He was due to speak at a fund-raising dinner on Monday. It was his first foray into public speaking since his illness.

He read his prepared speech and frowned. Surely he could do better.

He thought of Mardie and he thought…passion. The world could do with more passion. So could his speech.

He squared his shoulders and pulled up a blank document. Try again? He couldn't quite match Mardie in the passion stakes but he'd give it his best shot.

* * *

The sheep were as safe as she could make them. They had feed and water, the hens were happy, the place was secure.

Back in the house, she looked—tentatively—for Blake and was relieved when she realised he was upstairs. She could hear him on his computer. Working.

Good. He was out of her hair.

He wouldn't have the internet up there. She should have offered him access to her computer.

She might make the offer, she decided, but not until after dinner. She hauled a tuna bake from the freezer. A nice easy fix. Plus it would underscore what she'd yelled at Blake. Excellent.

She picked a lettuce and a couple of tomatoes from the veggie patch. Practically gourmet. Blake Maddock would be used to five-star restaurants. How would he react to defrosted tuna bake?

She really had yelled at him.

Maybe she'd overdone it, just a little.

She should call him down. Have a drink before dinner.

Maybe not. She was, she discovered, still seething.

She should check the weather forecast. She hit the internet and confirmed there was not a storm in sight. Excellent.

She went to close the computer and then…

A thought.

She just happened to type *Blake Maddock, Ophthalmologist.*

She'd never searched for him. For all these years, she'd never enquired. She hadn't wanted to know.

She wanted to know now.

Blake Maddock, Ophthalmologist. Enter.

She entered Africa.

She stared at the screen as if it had grown two heads.

For Blake was right in front of her, but not the Blake she knew. This was the face of some major foundation, Eyes For Africa. Blake as a professional.

Blake working in desperate conditions. Blake, surrounded by queues of kids. Blake operating. Blake standing in the background as a nurse removed bandages from a little boy's eyes. A clip of a documentary describing Blake's work.

On the front of the website there was a blurb for a black-tie dinner this coming Monday in Sydney. *Head of Eyes For Africa, Dr Blake Maddock, will be addressing...*

She'd known nothing.

This town knew everything there was to know about everyone. Surely...

No. Banksia Bay knew everything there was to know about its own, and Blake no longer belonged. His aunt had scorned the town, and when Blake left that was the end.

She read on, her head spinning as she flicked through screens of information.

He'd headed to Africa almost as soon as he'd finished his specialist training. His work there was groundbreaking.

He'd said he worked overseas. But...Africa? *All this time...*

'I guess you know all about me now, too,' Blake said from behind her and she froze. She didn't turn. To say she was dumbfounded would be an understatement.

'Africa,' she whispered.

'It's where I keep my harem. Stocked by my white slave traders.'

She managed a smile but it didn't reach her eyes. This was too astounding for humour.

'You work for charity,' she said, finally spinning to face him.

'Yes.'

'You're not rich.' It was...an accusation?

'I am,' he said diffidently. 'My family made a fortune in tin mining—I still own shares. My great-aunt had extravagant taste in home renovation but for the rest she was miserly. My parents died before they could spend their inheritance. I can afford to pay for a dog and a bit of tree clearing.'

'That's not what I meant,' she said, thoroughly confused. 'I thought you studied medicine to make money.'

'Why would I do that, when I already have far more than I need?'

'I don't know,' she said miserably. 'How would I know? Blake, why?'

The question was almost a wail.

'Does there have to be a why?'

'Yes,' she managed. 'There does. I thought I knew all about you. Then I thought I didn't know anything. Now...' She shook her head. 'Sorry. It has nothing to do with me, what you do. I don't have the right to ask.'

She closed her eyes. She counted to ten because she didn't know what else to do.

Opened them. Thought of a long-ago question.

Asked it.

'Who's Robbie?'

The question hung.

Robbie.

'Why—' he found it hard to speak '—why do you ask?'

There was a long silence. The question hung.

And then she told him, 'There was someone called Robbie.' It was a statement, not a question, and it left him winded.

There was someone called Robbie.

Not according to his parents. Or his great-aunt. No one.

There was someone called Robbie.

'Yes,' he said. 'How did you know?'

'It's the only thing I've been able to think of,' she said, sounding unsure. 'When you left...I thought I knew everything about you, my best of friends. But that last night... You were so excited about leaving, about studying medicine. But you'd never said what you wanted to do until then. It was like there was some part of you you'd kept hidden. I couldn't figure it out, but after you'd gone and I was trying to make sense of it…Robbie was the one thing I couldn't ask about. He was the one thing I didn't know.'

He tried to think of something to say. He couldn't.

'How…?' he managed again at last.

'When we camped out in the tent on the back lawn,' she said diffidently. Unsure. 'As kids. You cried out in your sleep. Nightmares. Stuff like "Robbie I can't… Robbie, don't…" I got Mum and she brought us both inside and cuddled you back to sleep. Then, another time when you were sleeping over, I heard you crying, "Robbie, Robbie", and I knew Mum went up to you. I asked you once, "Who's Robbie?" and you said no one. I asked Mum, and she said kids who lived alone often have friends in their head. She said if you didn't want to tell us then I wasn't to ask. But I thought… Whenever you had the dream…you sounded terrified. I heard Mum tell Dad once, "That boy has demons". For some reason when you left I thought…I thought the demons might be Robbie.'

Robbie.

For all these years he'd done what his father told him.

'Don't tell people about your brother. It makes your mother ill.'

And then, when he couldn't stop crying, he'd been packed off to Australia, to an aunt who barely said Blake's name, much less his twin's.

Robbie…

The sound of Mardie saying it was a release all by itself.

The demons might be Robbie. It was suddenly unbearable that she thought that a moment longer.

'Robbie was my brother,' he said, and the words sounded strange, as if they were coming from some dark recess that had been locked for years. They were.

'Your brother?'

'My twin.'

She was on the swivelling computer chair. The chair wasn't

moving. She was totally motionless, her eyes not leaving his. Trying to read him.

'He died?'

'Before I came here.'

'How old?' It was scarcely a whisper.

'When I was…when we were seven. We were living in a beachside mansion in California. My mother's birthday. A party, so many people. It was hot, we couldn't sleep so we decide to go for a swim.'

'Night?' she whispered.

'Midnight. It was a stupid time to go for a swim, but there was so much noise…'

'Your parents let you go for a swim at midnight?'

'They didn't know. We were supposed to be sleeping, but it was hot. And the nanny…' He shrugged. 'I don't know where she was. Anyway, we crept down the back stairs. The noise… I remember one woman was laughing like a hyena. Robbie copied her. He was giggling.' He paused. 'And then he dived into the pool, into the shallow end. His neck…'

He broke off. How to go further? He couldn't. Even to Mardie.

'Enough,' he said. 'It's ancient history. My parents never talked of him, didn't want me to talk of him. My aunt didn't speak of him either. That was fine by me. It hurt, so I didn't. But it seemed… When I got into medicine…'

'You did that for Robbie?'

'I did it for me,' he said savagely. 'To stop the hurting. I thought…if I could help kids…' He raked his hair. 'Sorry. I'm not going to burden you. Robbie's my shadow, and he's always with me. Working in Africa helps, makes up in some way for Robbie having a life. I know now that trying to forget him made it worse. It seemed a betrayal but I had no choice. I was a kid and decisions were made for me that were bad. I've moved on. Or maybe I'm still moving on.' He hesitated, regrouped, somehow hauled his thoughts back to now. 'Can I smell fish?'

'Tuna,' she said, looking stunned.

'Tuna bake?'

'Y…yes.'

'Excellent,' he said. 'My favourite.'

'Liar.'

'I don't lie,' he said and then he smiled. 'Okay, maybe I'm stretching the truth a little when it comes to tuna bake. How long is it that it's been frozen?'

They ate dinner in near silence. Tuna bake. What's not to like? Mardie thought, though maybe it was time she did a bit of freezer-clearing. Time had made the noodles crystallise, and even though they'd reheated looking fine, they tasted… well, cardboard might be a good way to describe them.

Even Bounce and Bessie seemed a bit dubious.

Thinking about clearing freezers was okay. Thinking about dogs was okay, too. If she thought about a seven-year-old called Robbie, her head might explode.

'You know, I reckon the dogs need to get used to these tuna bakes,' Blake said as he helped her clear. 'How many more do you have?'

She smiled, but absently, circling the subject of Robbie. Knowing she should go back to him. Thinking she couldn't.

She was feeling as if this man beside her was suddenly who she'd thought he was—a part of her. It was a dumb feeling, but there it was.

Blake… How she'd felt… How she was feeling… It was muddling into emotional turmoil.

She wanted to put her arms around him and hug him.

She wanted…

No.

'The internet said you're in Australia fund-raising,' she managed at last, cautiously.

'Yes.'

'When are you going back?'

'I'm not sure.'

'You're not…?'

'Is there anything else that needs doing? If not, I should get some work done before bed.'

She was finding it hard to speak. She'd known this man so well, once upon a time. How strange that Robbie, Africa, these two great unknowns about him, were making her feel that, at some deep level, he was still…hers?

He'd always kept his inner thoughts to himself, but she'd guessed stuff. She'd even guessed that someone called Robbie was important, but she'd accepted her mother's explanation.

And when he'd left? Hormones had messed with how she'd reacted, she thought. She'd been too busy seeing her needs, her loss, that she hadn't begun to probe what he needed.

Okay. She attempted an inner regroup. She did know this man. Pressing him for answers would never work. She needed to come at him sideways.

He'd asked her if anything needed doing. She met his gaze then, and for the first time she really looked at him. Really saw him. She was looking for the boy behind the man, the Blake she knew. She'd been disconcerted by his size, his deep, sexy voice, his dinner suit, his crashed Mercedes.

Now she just saw Blake.

And she saw the strain. Something lost. Something more than a long-ago grief.

He'd tell her in time, she thought. If she could regain a little of what was lost.

Okay, moving sideways… She looked down at her feet to where two dogs were slumped side by side. Alternate universe. Dogs.

'Bessie smells,' she said.

Blake looked startled. 'Sorry?'

'She's been lost for a week. Before that she was in the

pound. Tomorrow we're taking her to Sydney. My truck's a four-seater so she can sit in the back with Bounce, but it's going to be a pretty pongy journey.' She managed a grin. 'If it was Bounce I'd wait until a warm day and put the hose on him. Bessie, though, needs tenderness. That means warm water in the tub in the wash-house, towels and my hairdryer. You just asked if you could help. Here's your answer. I'm not sure how Bessie feels about personal hygiene but if she's anything like Bounce, heaven help us both. You hold and I'll wash. Let's go.'

The wash-house was a lean-to bathroom-cum-laundry at the back of the house. The bath was huge.

Mardie filled the bath, and Blake tried lifting Bessie in.

A lot of farmers never washed their dogs. They either made them stay outside or in some cases they were so used to smell-of-dog in their living room they didn't notice. Fleas were dealt with by dumping the dogs in the sheep dip.

Maybe that was all Bessie had known. It was certainly all she wanted to know. When Blake lowered her into the water she responded as if this was death-by-drowning.

'It's okay, it's okay, it's okay,' Mardie said, frantically soothing, but frantic and soothing didn't go together. Bessie opted simply for frantic. She lurched upwards, managed to get her paws onto Blake's shoulders and heaved.

Blake was suddenly prone, backwards on the floor, with sodden collie all over him.

Mardie tried hard to keep a straight face.

She failed.

'Oh, dear…' she said, convulsing.

'You try,' Blake said, staggering upright. Glowering. Dripping.

Mardie grinned. Excellent. Blake might be a highly trained eye surgeon, but this was her territory. She could wrangle a ram if she must. A gentle collie…

Nothing to it.

There was, actually, something to it. She ended up as soaked as Blake, but pride was at stake, and Bessie stayed put.

'Shampoo,' she said bracingly to Blake. 'You soap her.'

'I'm wet enough.'

'Wet doesn't stop the smell. Pull yourself together. A bit of willpower.'

'Right,' he said and staggered back to the fray. Laughing.

Things had changed. Something about wetness and laughter and a shared challenge. The tension of the past few hours peeled away.

Blake and Mardie and a dog. Two dogs, for Bounce was cautiously out of range, anxiously supervising as his new love was turned into a sudsy mop.

Things were suddenly okay again. Or more okay than they'd been.

They were back to…

Friends?

By now Bessie had figured they weren't trying to drown her. She'd figured suds meant no harm. So she settled. Except for the shaking.

She wasn't shaking from terror. She was shaking as an intelligent dog got rid of water. No matter how hard Mardie held, she sent suds flying all the way to Bounce at the door.

Blake was doing his best to massage the suds. Every time she shook he got coated.

Every time she shook Mardie subsided into giggles.

'It's fine for you; you have a change of clothes,' Blake retorted, massaging on with grim determination.

'I have a clothes dryer,' she said. 'It's not great for dinner suits but it's fine for work gear. You can go back into the bathrobe while I clean your clothes.'

'Domesticity at its finest,' he said dryly—and then chuckled.

She loved his chuckle. She loved… She loved…

Bessie chose that moment to shake again, which was just as well. Because suddenly Mardie wasn't sure what she loved. Or where the boundaries were.

The boundaries were deeply scary.

They dried Bessie as best they could in the sodden bathroom, then took her into the living room. They towelled her in front of the fire and Mardie fetched her hairdryer.

There was a moment's alarm from Bessie; hairdryers were also something she'd never met. But the warmth of the fire, Mardie's reassurances, Bounce's presence—Bounce knew what a hairdryer was and was intent on sharing the hot air himself—was enough to make her relax.

Mardie and Blake were wet but the room was warm, and what was a little damp between friends? They sat by the fire, with Bessie draped over their knees, Mardie drying and combing, and Blake cutting tangles.

They worked in silence, but the silence wasn't tense. It was as if they were getting to know each other all over again.

Coming together. Merging.

They swapped ends and worked on.

Bessie relaxed completely. She was warm and cared for and the safest she'd been since she'd been put in the pound. She practically purred.

'I hate the thought of taking her to Sydney,' Mardie murmured. She was drying her tail, a lovely feathery black-and-white wag machine. 'Uprooting her again seems cruel. I just want to let her settle.'

'She can't get what she needs in Banksia Bay.'

'Same as you?'

'This was never my home,' he said simply.

'So where's home now?'

No answer. She didn't press.

They finished drying. Bounce gave Bessie an encouraging lick, as if to say, *Job done, wake up, your place is with me now.*

Bessie heaved herself to her feet. Bounce waited until she was steady, then headed for the sofa.

The living room sofa was forbidden to dogs except on the rare occasions when Mardie needed comfort, or when a dog could sidle in unnoticed and curl up before Mardie saw...

Bounce edged to the sofa, Bessie by his side. He glanced nervously at Mardie—and then he was up, Bessie with him.

The two dogs were practically grinning as they dived between cushions. They wriggled under, and hid. Not very well.

Mardie should yell.

It was all she could do not to laugh.

'I take it by Bounce's demeanour that the sofa's forbidden,' Blake said, smiling with her.

'It certainly is. I'm sure Bessie knows it, too.'

She must. Both dogs had nosed under cushions, determined on invisible.

Mardie giggled. She felt...

As if she was standing on the edge of something momentous. Huge.

How she felt about Blake.

'We're both wet,' Blake said, sounding regretful. 'I need to get these clothes into the dryer.'

That'd mean going to bed. They both knew it.

Neither of them moved.

The fire was crackling, sending out gentle heat. They weren't cold. Wet or not, staying right here seemed an excellent option.

She was like the dogs, Mardie thought. She was blocking out the world, revelling in comfort, hoping she wouldn't be noticed.

She was taking comfort from Blake's presence, hoping it wouldn't end.

'Tell me what Hugh was like,' Blake said softly and it had ended.

Or...not, she thought, confused. It should hurt, telling this man about the man who'd been her husband, but suddenly it didn't.

It seemed right.

'Hugh was my friend,' she said softly. 'He was ten years older than me. He was big and quiet and solid. He laughed when I did. I loved him.'

'Would I have liked him?'

'He wasn't like you.'

'That's not what I asked.'

'No.' She considered.

Hugh. A man supremely contented with his lot.

He was the youngest of seven brothers. He'd been brought up tough.

He didn't have an ounce of toughness in him.

He had the best smile.

'Yes, you would have liked him,' she said and she knew it was true. And then she thought...if Hugh could see her now, curled up by the fire, covered in dog hair, smelling of dog shampoo, talking to her friend from childhood...

'He would have liked you, too,' she said. 'He'd be glad, for me, that you're here. I used to tell him about you. He liked it. He didn't have all that happy a childhood himself and he was hungry for happy.' She hesitated. 'He would have been really interested in what you do. "Tell me," he'd say. So that's what I'm saying. Tell me about Africa.'

He hesitated. Unsure. 'I suspect you've read all you need to know,' he said diffidently.

She thought about that, of the countless documentaries she'd seen, of the wildlife, of the humanitarian crises, the sheer scope of human tragedy.

Yes, she'd read about it. But to be there...

'What does it smell like?'

'Smell…'

'Smell. First impression.'

'Dry and sparse and wind-blown,' he said, frowning. 'I used to stand on the cliffs here and smell the salt. In Africa I smell the sand. The wind… The locals call it *arifi*, meaning thirst, a wind that scorches with many tongues. It rips the heart out of a man. It doesn't give a smell, it takes it away. It leaves you sucked dry. And the people…the kids…the damage…' His voice died. 'There's no point thinking about it.'

'You're doing something about it.'

'Not any more.'

'You're not going back?' she asked, astounded all over again.

'Not,' he said harshly, feeling the frustration build. 'I can't. I might be forced to go back to something like you're doing.'

'Um…' she said cautiously, stunned by his sudden anger. 'Are we back where we started? Mardie Rainey, born in Banksia Bay, headstone for the local cemetery ordered at the same time as my birth certificate?'

'I didn't mean…'

'I'm sure you did mean.' She might be shocked into sympathy but she wasn't letting him get away with this. 'You're summing up my life as worthless?'

'I didn't…'

'Yes, you did,' she said, but she wasn't angry. She was simply sad. 'How do you think that could make me feel?' she said, meeting his gaze square on. 'Seeing my husband die and watching my mother fade. Living here by myself, in my childhood home, and then opening the door to my ex-best friend who tells me what a waste my life has been. You're right, I haven't saved a single African child. We all can't.' Deep breath. 'Why do you keep trying to hurt me?'

'I'm not.'

'I believe you are,' she said steadily. 'I thought…I thought I didn't know you any more but it seems I do. I remember when Mum used to try and hug you, you'd turn yourself rigid, pushing her away. It took her ages to be able to hug. I think you're doing exactly the same thing now. Why?'

'Are you trying to hug?'

'I'm not trying to hug,' she said simply. 'I'm asking what's wrong. One friend to another. You've told me about Robbie. Now tell me about the next big thing. The thing that's put the strain behind your eyes. The thing that's making you want to lash out.'

'I…'

'Just say it, Blake,' she said softly. She put out her hand and touched his—and she waited.

For however long it took.

The fire crackled in the grate. Bounce started snoring. Bessie wuffled and nudged cushions so the two dogs were closer.

She waited.

And finally he closed his eyes and said it.

'I can't go back to Africa,' he said, and he tugged his hand from hers, as if he no longer had the right to the contact. 'It seems I'm taking my frustration out in all sorts of inappropriate ways. It seems hurting you is one of them.'

'Why not?' she said at last.

'I've had dengue fever three times. They tell me three strikes and I'm out. I've had my three strikes.'

'You can never go back?'

'Nowhere there's dengue'

'Or you die?'

'I know the odds. I believe them.'

'So what will you do?' She managed a half smile. 'Unless you're serious about running sheep?'

He shrugged, not returning her smile. 'Who knows? Feel sorry for myself. Go to school reunions. Hurt my friends.'

'There's three strikes,' she said. 'You've done them all. Now you're out again. So the next thing is…'

'I have no idea.'

She thought for a little. Thought about touching his hand again. Thought better of it.

The fire did some more crackling. Bounce did some more snoring. Bessie just seemed to…listen.

There was no hurry for what had to be said.

'Burying yourself in anger would be the fourth thing,' she said at last. 'When Hugh died, I yelled at trees, at rocks, at my friends, at the kids who crashed into us, at anything. It didn't help.'

'Neither did anyone telling you to get over it.'

She smiled at that, wryly. Agreed with a vengeance. 'All that did was make me want to slug someone even worse. Like I wanted to slug you when you criticised me.'

'So now it's you who's angry?'

'Maybe I am,' she said. 'Why wouldn't I be angry? You're judging my life as worth less than yours. You're saying if you can't go to Africa you're nothing. But you can't see what I get and what I give.' She met his eyes, challenging. 'I like my life, and I do good things. I make people happy. I make me happy and I don't need to defend myself to you or to anyone.'

'I know you don't.'

'Then stop beating yourself up about something you can't change. You do the best you can. No one should expect you to do more than that, including the ghost of Robbie, including yourself.' She hesitated. She wanted, quite badly, to take his face in her hands and kiss him. As comfort?

If it was only that, she thought, she'd do it in a heartbeat, but there was that between them…

'Go to bed, Blake,' she said instead. 'Relax. Think of all the excellent things you can do in the world. There's lots, I'm sure there are, in places where there isn't dengue. Figure it out.'

She pushed herself to her feet.

He rose with her. Came too fast.

She was too close.

His hands came out and steadied her.

And the need grew.

A need from fifteen years ago?

That night in the kitchen…a kiss interrupted. It was between them now, a tangible thing. Fifteen years and a kiss unfinished.

Fifteen years of need.

A need that was as great now as it had been then. More so.

A need that seemed a compulsion, an aching void that had to be filled.

Two halves of a whole, meant to be together.

The fire hissed at their feet, sap catching, making tiny explosions, fizzing to nothing.

A need so great…

'Do you want me to kiss you?' Blake asked, and the world held its breath. The world including Mardie.

'Properly?' she asked.

'With your mother not watching.' He was smiling, a smile that turned her heart.

'I've spent fifteen years figuring out how that kiss should have ended,' she whispered, trying to keep her voice steady. 'I wouldn't mind knowing…'

She wouldn't mind knowing what?

He had no chance to find out because he was no longer listening.

A prophecy carved in a ruined tree. *M.R. xx B.M.* Carved when she was ten years old.

Finally happening.

And fifteen years were gone, just like that. They were a man and a woman grown, but at some basic level they were still who they'd been, friends who'd spent half a lifetime together, who'd grown from boy and girl to man and woman, and who'd moved to this, the next and natural level.

It felt natural. It felt inevitable and it felt right.

Her lips melted against his. Her body curved into his, and she moulded into his hold, tilting her chin, taking as well as giving.

He tasted her kiss.

He tasted her mouth.

He tasted her body and he loved her, as he always had, as he always would.

She smelled of dog shampoo. In truth, maybe she tasted of dog shampoo.

She was wonderfully, miraculously perfect.

She was Mardie. His friend. His home.

She was too great a temptation to resist. She was too sweet to think of pulling away.

She was too much his Mardie to do anything but kiss her.

For this moment he surrendered absolutely. He let himself hold her as he wanted to hold her, to be in this place, by her fire with her dogs nearby, to have her in his arms and to feel her loving him.

Mardie of the loving heart…

He'd fallen in love in the school playground all those years ago and he'd never fallen out. He loved her with every shred of his being.

Forget the dog shampoo. She tasted of nectar, ambrosia, more. She tasted…

Of Mardie

Mardie. His Mardie.

He hadn't known he was off centre but he knew it now. Mardie. His centre.

She was on tiptoe, deepening the kiss, demanding as well as giving. Surrendering but besieging. Wanting as much as he wanted.

She wasn't close enough. He was tugging her against him,

her breasts were curved into his chest and she felt as if she was melting into him.

He wanted her closer.

Part of him.

Her hands were in the small of his back, clinging. He was still damp. The fabric between them felt as if it was nothing. There was only a vestige of decency.

The vestige of sense...

He couldn't think that.

But...he had to think it or he'd sweep her up and take her to bed, this instant. It was all he wanted to do. For it felt so right, so meant. After fifteen years, finding his home.

Her hands were slipping to his hips. Tugging him closer still.

Sense.

All he wanted was to take her. All he wanted was to give.

Sense!

Somehow he found the strength to pull away, to break the contact, and heaven knew it broke more than that.

He did it. He held her by her shoulders, at arm's length, gazing down into her dazed and bewildered eyes.

'Blake...' she whispered and her hands covered his. 'You don't want...'

'I did want,' he managed in a voice he scarcely recognised. 'I do want. But I should never... I can't have.'

'Why can't you have?' There was suddenly a trace of indignation in her voice, the feisty Mardie surfacing under the lover. 'It's not as if I'm unavailable,' she said. 'Is it the thought of Hugh?'

She was suddenly glaring at him. Self-sacrifice, it seemed, wasn't in her vocabulary. He wanted to smile.

He didn't.

He'd wanted to kiss her and he had, but now...he felt as if he was at the edge of a deep, sweet vortex, being tugged inexorably into its unknown centre.

Away from everything he'd worked for.

'I'm not giving up,' he said, hardly aware he was speaking. 'I can't. To escape back to Banksia Bay... I no longer need to escape.'

She tugged back so his hands could no longer hold her shoulders. She looked confused. But then his gaze locked on hers and there was anger behind the confusion. Anger growing.

It seemed she was waiting for an explanation. It was as if he'd kissed her under false pretences.

Suddenly she was practically tapping her foot.

So explain. If he could.

'Mardie, my parents sent me here after Robbie died because it made my mother ill to look at me,' he said, trying hard to make sense of what he hardly understood himself. 'My great-aunt took me in. This place had been her refuge for years and it became mine. My parents were...dysfunctional, to say the least. My great-aunt was little better, but once I met you, and your parents... This was safe as I'd never been safe. It was home as nowhere had ever been home. Even after ten years here I still felt overwhelming thankfulness that I'd found you. I could have stayed. But I had things to do, my Mardie-girl. I still have things to do, and I can't do them here.'

'Don't call me Mardie-girl.'

Mardie-girl.

He hadn't meant to.

Her father had called her Mardie-girl, and in private, as they'd grown older, it had started slipping out. Mardie. His Mardie-girl. No. She was right. Its use now was inappropriate.

And it had rekindled anger.

'I'm only Mardie-girl to people I love,' she snapped—but then she flinched and she closed her eyes. 'Though that's dumb,' she whispered. 'Because I do love you. You know I always have. Though not...not like this. Not like tonight. What

I had with Hugh was real and wonderful, and the thought of you didn't get in the way for a moment. But we've always... meshed. Only I never saw myself as a safe harbour. An escape. I saw myself as an equal. A friend. Fun, happy, silly, sad—you and me, mates.'

'We were. I hope we are.'

'Then why are you spouting nonsense about escape?'

'I don't know that, either.' He raked his hair and raked it again for good measure.

'Then I guess that makes two of us not understanding,' she said, more mildly now. 'I thought you wanted to kiss me. It seems I was wrong. Okay. You've stopped kissing me, so let's leave it at that. You need to strip off and put those clothes in the dryer. You can't do that with me around. I might get the wrong idea. No. That's nuts. It's all nuts. I'm confused, you're confused. So let's focus on what we know for sure. We have two happy dogs, one of whom needs medical help. Tomorrow we're going to Sydney. So tonight I'll leave you to your convolutions and your plans for the future, which doesn't include kissing, and I'll go to bed. Goodnight, Blake. Happy plans.'

And that was that. She clicked her fingers for the dogs and she headed out of the room and down the passage to her bedroom.

She walked inside, the dogs following her—side by side, Bounce glancing back at him with what looked like reproach—and she slammed the door behind them.

She left and he stood by the fire until it died to embers.

Once again he'd hurt her. He should walk away now.

She was driving him to Sydney. She'd have to put up with him the whole way. She'd see him during the week as they cared for Bessie. Then...

Did he really want to walk away?

No. But what was between them...

It wasn't friendship. It was so much more.

That she'd guessed about Robbie left him winded. That she and her parents had respected his privacy, had guessed he was hurting, had let him be…that left him awed.

They'd loved him.

Love. It was a strange concept.

In medical school he'd met a girl as committed to aid organisations as he was, passionate about saving the world. They'd studied together, worked together, become lovers almost as a side issue. Become engaged.

Six months later she'd met an African aid worker and fell hopelessly, helplessly in love. 'I'm sorry, Blake, it's the way he makes me feel. I really love him.'

They were still friends. But…love?

The way a heart twisted?

The way he makes me feel…

The way he felt tonight, when he'd held Mardie.

No. Stop, right now. This is Banksia Bay.

Banksia Bay was never an option.

He didn't think Mardie's life was worthless, of course he didn't, but…could he imagine himself working here? Taking care of coughs and colds? Playing with sheep on the side?

Being with Mardie-girl.

Just Mardie, he corrected himself. Not his Mardie-girl. What had once been granted to him with love, had now been withdrawn.

He couldn't pursue it.

Because of Robbie? He'd forgiven himself years ago for Robbie's death. One seven-year-old could never be held responsible for another's moment of risk-taking, regardless of what his mother had thought and said. But still that sense remained, to do something worthwhile, to somehow compensate for the waste that was his brother.

He should be able to walk away from it. See a shrink. Move on.

But it had been with him for too long, was too great a part of his life. He had no hope of ever moving on.

And that meant walking away from Mardie? He knew it did.

The door swung open, almost of its own accord. He glanced across and it was Bessie. She'd managed to push past the loosely hinged doors. For some reason she was nosing her way across to him, following his scent. Finding him. Putting a paw up, as if asking for a pat.

As if offering comfort.

He'd always wanted a dog. He'd always been so jealous of Mardie and her dog pack.

If he stayed here…

No.

'You don't belong with me,' he told Bessie, more roughly than he intended. 'Bounce is just down the hall. So's Mardie.' And before he could think further about it he led her out of the room, down the passage.

Mardie's door was open. Bessie must have pushed it wide again.

He could just call…

He didn't.

He propelled Bessie silently into the room and closed the door after her.

And went up to bed without saying a word.

She heard him return Bessie

She heard him close the door.

She lay awake and thought.

About two little boys swimming at midnight. About Blake's parents. Packing him off to Australia. Loading him with guilt. The legacy they'd given their son…

Anger was no use.

That was the problem. Nothing was any use. What had

been done was done, and Blake was living with the consequences for ever.

It was doing her head in. Anger, sorrow—there was even a touch of humiliation tossed in there as well. She had it all.

She thought and thought, until sleep finally gave her release.

She dreamed of twins.

She dreamed of Blake.

She woke to the sounds of chopping.

Blake. Doing his manly thing again. Sigh.

At least it wasn't the chainsaw, she thought grimly, throwing back the covers and heading for the window.

The first weak rays of dawn were barely filtering over the horizon. Even Clarabelle wasn't at the gate yet.

Blake was chopping.

He was back in his jeans, but he was bare to the waist. He was lifting the logs he'd sectioned yesterday, putting them on the block beside the woodshed and attacking. The axe came down over and over, with strong, rhythmic strokes.

The wood was green. It took three, four strokes to strike each log through.

He didn't falter. One after another. Stacking the pieces and moving to the next. No pause.

She should call out that she had enough wood to last her for the winter. She wouldn't be burning it green anyway, and next winter it'd split with half the effort.

But she knew without being told that he needed the physical effort.

Demons. Her mother had surely been right.

Not demons. Robbie.

He didn't look up. Every ounce of energy went into smashing the axe into the wood.

She wanted to walk out and take the axe from him. She wanted to hold him, just hold him, the child inside the man.

She couldn't. Whatever harm his parents had caused had gone so deep she couldn't touch. His harm would just hurt her.

Fifteen years ago he'd walked away and she'd lived without him ever since. She could do it again.

With demons like his, there didn't seem a choice.

CHAPTER SEVEN

THE journey to Sydney was made mostly in silence. The truck had an excellent radio, for which Mardie was profoundly thankful. She tuned it to a discussion on nineteenth-century circuses. She tried to be fascinated.

For Blake had gone somewhere she couldn't reach. He was silent and grim, hardly speaking at all.

'Hitchhikers are supposed to entertain the truckies who pick 'em up,' she said at one stage.

'Would you like me to talk?'

'I'd like you to tell me about Africa,' she suggested. 'More than it has a truly appalling wind.'

'You don't want to know.'

'Fine, then,' she said, grittily cheerful, and went back to her circuses.

When they reached the city she needed facts. 'Where's your apartment? Where can I drop you off?'

'It's on the harbour,' he said shortly. 'But you don't want to be caught in city traffic, and we need to take Bessie to the vet clinic. We'll go to your place, dump your stuff and take her straight there.'

'Yes, sir.'

'I didn't mean...'

'To be brusque? Of course you did,' she retorted. 'But I like brusque. Least said, soonest parted. Let's go.'

* * *

Least said, soonest parted… He wouldn't have put it like that, but then he wouldn't have put it at all. He was simply doing what he needed to do.

If he told her what he thought of the pompous historian spouting circus stuff, if he joined in, he might relax, and if he relaxed then they'd end up where they were last night and he'd end up hurting her. Hurting her more.

Shut up and move on. Do what needs to be done. Leave.

To go where?

He'd figure it. Eventually.

'This is Irena's,' Mardie said, pulling up outside a tiny weatherboard cottage overlooking the cliffs of Coogee. 'She has cats. Bounce is used to them. Let's see how Bessie reacts.'

He climbed from the truck as Mardie negotiated the garden path and rang the bell.

Irena's house. A friend of Mardie's. If he'd thought about it, he'd probably have guessed Irena to be a Banksia Bay local who'd moved on.

Country girl made good?

That was the kind of thinking that was getting him into trouble.

It might also be a little bit wrong.

For the woman who opened the door was…magnificent. Fiftyish. Six feet tall. Black leggings, high black boots, a purple sweater that reached mid-thigh and a tiny skirt. Strings of amethyst and topaz. Oversized earrings.

A Cleopatra haircut.

She greeted Mardie with a cry of delight, enveloped her in a hug and Mardie practically disappeared.

The hug over, Mardie was held at arm's length and inspected.

'Look at you.' It was a cry of dismay. 'If you haven't brought anything decent to wear…'

'I have brought clothes but I don't want to get dog on them.

Irena, meet Blake Maddock, the guy I was telling you about. Blake, Irena's my agent.'

Her agent?

'How lovely,' Irena purred, and smiled a totally bewitching smile that said she knew exactly what personable men were made for and she knew exactly what to do with them.

Mardie giggled. 'You're scaring him,' she said.

'Not him. He's a big boy.' She grinned at Blake and turned back to Mardie. 'Did you bring them?'

'Yes, but…'

'I want to see them. Now.'

'We need to get Bessie to the vet's.'

'Colin's not expecting us for another hour.' Blake was fascinated.

'An hour's great,' Irena said with satisfaction. 'And you said it's right by here. Excellent. Bring them in.'

'The dogs…?' Blake ventured.

'Bring them in, too,' Irena said with ill-concealed impatience. And then she gave a rueful smile. 'Sorry. Your dog's why we're getting the plates early and I should be grateful. I am. So I'll take Bounce inside, and the memory box—is it in the tray? Mardie, you bring Bessie and introduce her to the girls. Blake, you bring the plates.'

'The plates?'

'It's the box on the back seat,' Mardie said, taking pity on him. 'The memory box is the big one in the tray. The plates are smaller. But please be careful. If you drop them I'll have to shoot myself.'

'You and me both,' Irena said. 'And Cathy.' She glanced at her watch. 'I hope you don't mind but she's been desperate to see. She should be here… Oh, great, here she is now. Come on in.'

And then they were in Irena's huge kitchen, which seemed to take up half the house. There were two Siamese cats, circling the dogs with care. Bessie seemed cautious but not over-whelmed. She stuck close to Bounce and seemed fine.

It was Cathy who looked overwhelmed.

Cathy was a middle-aged woman, mousy, wearing a twin-set and a tweed skirt, looking scared. She'd received one of Irena's hugs as well, which could, Blake thought, overwhelm anyone.

'Blake doesn't know what's happening,' Mardie announced, looking bemused. 'Sorry, Blake, I should have told you.'

'You didn't tell him about the memory wall?' Irena demanded. 'It's only the most beautiful thing you've ever done.'

'Blake and I have been too busy for chat.' She was open-ing what Irena was calling the memory box. Tugging out as-sorted…things.

A battered seaman's cap. A container of model trains. A box of fishing flies. Photographs. Letters. Boots. An ancient pair of scuffed slippers.

A rat-trap?

What the…?

'Cathy's husband was drowned when a pilot boat tipped at the harbour mouth twelve months ago,' Irena told him and Cathy flinched as all eyes turned to her. She reached out and took the rat-trap, and held it as if it were a shield.

'I'm so sorry,' Blake said, because there was nothing else to say. 'What happened?'

'It was an awful night,' Mardie explained, as Cathy hugged her rat-trap like a talisman. 'An oil tanker was threatening to flounder on the rocks past the heads. They sent tugs and pilot boats out. They saved the tanker, but one of the tugs and one of the pilot boats were lost. Six men and two women were drowned. Cathy's Bernard was one of them.'

'Bernie was a crewman on the pilot boat,' Cathy whis-pered. 'He went out…and he didn't come back. It's been awful. But now…we're going to have a memorial wall, at the harbour where their boat used to be tied. Mardie's making plates. Nine plates for each one lost. Seventy-two plates in all. Mardie asked me to choose things that were important to Bernard, things the kids and I want him remembered for. Funny things. Silly things. Like the rat-trap.'

'Why the rat-trap?' Blake was totally caught in the emotion in the woman's face. The grief. The pride.

'We were friends at school,' she whispered, and pride prevailed. 'One day I told him there'd been a rat in my bedroom and the very next day Bernie brought me a rat-trap. We were both fourteen and I went to bed that night with my trap under the pillow. No way was I using it for rats.' She hesitated. 'Isn't it dumb, to have kept a rat-trap. Did…did you use it, Mardie?'

'I surely did,' Mardie said. 'Can you unpack the plates?' she asked him. 'Each panel's on individual padding.'

He lifted the plates free, one after another.

Nine enamelled plates.

He couldn't believe their beauty.

Each one was about twelve inches square.

The first was a portrait, glass, fired onto a copper base. A seaman.

It wasn't exactly a portrait, he thought. It was slightly abstract, an impression, but it was wonderful. The strength of the man came through—a battered sailor, his face creased against the weather, the sea behind him.

Cathy choked back a sob. She let the rat-trap fall to take it. She just…looked.

He lifted the next plate free. It was like a collage. A thing of exquisite beauty, but built from images of ordinariness. Here was the rat-trap. A football. Fishing flies.

A second plate was trains—a whole panel of trains Bernard had obviously loved. The real trains, the models, were spilling from the memory box, but their image on the plate was just as real. Bernard's face was on this plate again, as a faded background, a man watching with pride as his trains circled a track of crimson glass.

The colours were extraordinary. The depth of field, the layering of objects upon objects. Each one was saying this man had such depth...

Nine plates, representing a man's life.

Cathy was crying openly now, moving from plate to plate, touching them with awe, with reverence and with love.

'You guys need to get Bessie to the vet,' Irena said, a bit more roughly than she needed to, sniffing a bit, but Blake wasn't ready to surface yet.

He turned to Mardie—who was watching Cathy. Smiling a smile he'd never seen before.

'You did all these?' he managed.

'I've done seven sets,' she said. 'Sixty-three plates. I have Robyn Partling's story left to do. Another month and I'll be finished.'

'You should see where they're going,' Cathy whispered. 'They've made a wall at the harbour. Every person will see my Bernard. They'll see he loved trains. They'll see that letter he wrote to the paper about the turtles. They'll even see my rat-trap.'

She choked, and Irena put a bracing arm around her.

'Whisky,' she decreed. She turned to Mardie and Blake and sent them a silent message. Go. 'I'll dry Cathy up, but I suspect she'll like to be alone with these. So off you go and save your dog. Cathy and I will phone the harbour master. He's the one organising this. The other six have blown him away. This one will be no different.'

It took ten minutes to drive to the vet's. It took almost that long for Blake to catch his breath.

He remembered the plates over the fire-stove and knew now where they'd come from.

He'd seen the plate in Charlie's nursing-home bedroom and knew it was Mardie's as well.

Brilliant.

They pulled into the car park. Mardie went to get out of the truck but he caught her hand. There were things he needed to get clear.

'I always knew you could draw,' he said slowly. 'I never dreamed…'

'That I'd do enamelling? There you go, then. And I never dreamed you could be a doctor in Africa.'

'You never said…'

'You knew I loved drawing.'

'Yes, but not like this,' he said explosively. 'These plates… I'm not an expert but…with your skill you could make a fortune.'

'I do make money,' she said diffidently. 'But not with these. My friend Liz is a nurse I work with. Liz's brother, Mike, was one of the men who died that night. I came to the memorial service. I saw Liz clutching an old fire engine Mike loved when he was a kid and I thought…I could do something.'

'But you've been enamelling before?'

'For years. I run the sheep to keep the grass down. I work three days a week at the nursing home because I love it. The rest of the time I do this.'

'Raff said you were broke.' He was trying to get things clear. 'You couldn't afford to help Bessie. I assumed…'

'There's a lot of that about,' she said. 'Assumptions. You always saw my art as my hobby, not the passion it is. While I had no idea you were striving for medicine and why.'

'So you've been enamelling since school?'

'It's what I do,' she said gently. 'I don't make millions but I do make a living. The problem is the cost. There's always something. For these plates I needed a bigger kiln, a good one. You need an even temperature over the entire surface or the glass cracks. Lorraine's a local potter. She and I went halves but it still cost a fortune.'

She turned to Bessie and Bounce on the back seat, moving on with decision. The two dogs were sitting bolt upright in their harnesses, both looking nervous. 'Okay, Bessie, you're next. Do you think we should take Bounce in?'

'I think we should,' Blake said, because a man had to say something and that was all he could think of.

Concentrate on the dogs.

Anything else was too difficult.

Colin was waiting for them, a big, confident vet who oozed professional competence. In the veterinary clinic, with its strange smells, Bessie reacted with even more nervousness. Colin, however, was amenable to Bounce staying beside her. He could see that together they were settled.

A bond was growing between these two dogs that was starting to seem a tangible force.

Like me and Blake, Mardie thought, and scared herself by thinking it. Glanced at Blake and thought...for once, don't know what I'm thinking.

Luckily, both Colin and Blake were intent on Bessie's eyes. Colin was cautiously optimistic and once he examined her he became even more so.

'It's looking good. We'll need blood tests, scans, the works, and I need to start her on anti-inflammatory eye-drops. Can you leave her with me today, pick her up about five?'

'Can Bounce stay with her?' Mardie asked, and Bounce looked up with sudden distrust. 'I know, smarty-boots,' she told him. 'You understand. But today you're the sacrificial lamb. If I could hop into the cage with Bessie to comfort her I'd do it in a heartbeat, but I suspect I wouldn't fit.'

Everyone laughed

They left the dogs and walked out into the sunshine.

Laughter died. Silence.

No dogs. Nothing.

Sunshine, beach, nothing.

Without speaking, they headed towards the beach. Found themselves on the sand. Just walking.

Just walking.

There was something about Bessie and Bounce...

Togetherness. He hadn't felt like that even when he was engaged to be married.

Maybe that was why he was no longer engaged. He didn't know how to do it.

So what was the problem with that? He'd always been an outsider.

Except when he was with Mardie.

He was with Mardie now.

The difference was, Bessie and Bounce connected. They belonged together, in a way he and Mardie never could. Mardie had been his escape from reality. Banksia Bay. Mardie. They were part of his past, the part that had been used to 'get over Robbie'. Neither were part of his real world.

He could, Blake realised, walk away right now. He could pay Colin's bill. Take a cab into the city to his apartment. Leave Mardie with Irena, with her life that didn't include him.

No. There was a growing part of him that was denying his outsider tag, that was hungry to come in.

'I'd like to talk over what Colin says this afternoon,' he said diffidently. 'I have this fund-raising dinner tonight...'

Don't go any further. A voice was raging in his head. Don't! To be an outsider was the life he was accustomed to, the life he'd chosen.

A life where the pain of losing Robbie could never be repeated.

'Talking to lots of strangers,' Mardie said sympathetically. 'Ugh.'

'Would you like to come?'

He couldn't believe he'd said it.

He'd said it.

'It won't be all that interesting,' he said. 'Corporate money, politicians, people wanting to look charitable while contributing as little as possible. But…' He hesitated. 'You did ask about Africa.'

'So I did,' she said. 'You'll be talking about Africa?'

'Yes.'

'Then I'll come.'

Just like that. She glanced at him and their gazes locked— and then they looked away. A step taken…

Regretted?

'I'd like to be there, but inconspicuously,' she said hastily. 'Can you arrange for me to slip in at the back?' She ventured an uncertain smile. 'But, as for coming… It's only fair. You've seen my plates; I wouldn't mind seeing your work.'

'Great. I'll pick you up at…'

'No,' she said, suddenly definite. 'I have a truck. You have a mangled Mercedes. And, besides, I'm not coming as your partner. I'm coming as me. If you could organise a ticket I'll collect it at the door.'

'And you'll wear beige and blend into the wallpaper.'

'Something like that.'

'You're not an inconspicuous woman.'

'I am, too,' she said. 'Five feet two in socks. Favourite footwear, gumboots. Favourite perfume, wet dog.'

'In this crowd that'd be conspicuous,' he said and grinned. Feeling suddenly absurdly happy. Not knowing why but suddenly not caring. 'Would you like to have lunch now?' he asked before he knew he was going to.

But she was shaking her head. Looking a little…scared? 'Irena wants me to talk to the harbour master,' she told him. 'And I imagine you have things to do as well. If we need to discuss Bessie… Ring me in the morning if you don't get a chance to speak to me tonight.'

'Of course I'll get a chance.'

'It doesn't matter if you don't,' she said softly. 'We live in different worlds, Blake. They've collided today and it's lovely. But, apart from this one collision…we both need to get on with our lives.'

He did have things to do.

There was the small matter of insurance and a crumpled Mercedes. That took most of the afternoon.

He checked the cost of hiring another. Crashing hire cars did appalling things to premiums.

He gave up, found a car yard and bought one.

He headed back to his apartment. Ran through his presentation.

Passion.

He rewrote and rewrote. Thinking of Mardie.

Tell me about Africa…

What was she doing now?

She was due to pick the dogs up at five. She had a cellphone. He'd ring…

She answered on the second ring, and he thought: how easy was that? He could have rung her any time over the past fifteen years.

Why hadn't he?

He knew why.

'We're on the beach.' She was yelling into the wind. 'The dogs have spent all day in a cage. They have energy to spare.'

He wanted to be with them. Badly.

Not happening.

'How's Bessie coping?'

'She's running with Bounce, still just touching, but they're going as fast as each other. They look fabulous. I think they're in love.'

Love.

Don't go there.

Mardie would look fabulous too, he thought. Her hair would be flying every which way. She'd have bare feet, he guessed. Jeans, T-shirt, freckles, curls…

He was standing in his great-aunt's faded apartment.

He wanted to be on the beach with Mardie.

'What did Colin say?' he managed.

'He'll have the results of the blood tests back on Wednesday. There's a couple of other things, but he's really optimistic.' She hesitated. 'He's willing to do both eyes at once, if you'd like.'

'It's not up to me.'

'It is, because you're paying.'

'So pros and cons?' His emotions were all over the place. He seized on the professional with gratitude.

'It's cheapest to do one eye only,' she said. 'Dogs manage well with one eye.'

'They manage better with two. But if there's infection…'

'He said that. He said if he operates on two at once there's a tiny chance of cross infection; that something going wrong with one can mess with the other. But he says the chances are minuscule; he's almost willing to guarantee success in a dog as young and healthy as Bess. And here's the thing. He also says it wouldn't put her under additional stress. She'd have it done, it'd be over, I could take her home and she never need come here again.'

Excellent. But why did that make him feel…wrong?

'So that's that, then,' he said, more harshly than he intended. 'Two eyes. Decision made. Are you still coming tonight?'

'I… Yes, if it's okay.'

'I've organised a ticket.'

'I'll come just as the dinner ends,' she said. 'I'd like to hear you speak but you don't need to pay for my dinner.'

'Speeches are through dinner. There's no choice.'

'Then can I have a nice quiet seat down the back where I can sneak away?'

'It's all arranged,' he said. 'I'll see you then.'

'Then I'd best go and get the sand out from between my toes,' she said. 'Oo-er. And I just bet Irena will make me put on a frock.'

The dinner was formal. Very formal.

If Mardie had known how much the tickets cost, she'd never have agreed to come, Blake thought, as he greeted what seemed like the complete *Who's Who* of Australia. Politicians. Celebrities. There were a few professionals who were here to learn, like the doctors from North Coast Rescue—a division of the Australian Flying Doctor service—but they were in the minority. Most people were here to see and be seen.

Maybe he should have warned her. Even sneaking into a dark corner, she wouldn't want to look like a country mouse.

She *was* a country mouse.

She was also one of the most brilliant artists he'd ever met. Mardie.

He felt like shouting it to the rooftops. Hey. The Mardie I knew… The Mardie I disparaged… She's kind and loyal and clever—and she's talented beyond belief.

She was nothing to do with him.

One of the most eminent politicians in the land was waiting to be introduced. He needed to get a grip. Work the room. Remember why he was here.

'I'm very happy to meet you, ma'am. We certainly appreciate what you've done for us. Let me tell you about Sharik. She's five years old—here's her photograph. Through your funding, she can now see. If I could just tell you about the rest of the children in her village…'

* * *

She hadn't thought this through.

They had fund-raising dinners at Banksia Bay. Yes, she knew it'd be a bigger deal than that, but this... This was breathtaking.

The venue was right on Sydney Harbour. There were queues of cars lining up. Rollers. Bentleys. Porsches. A Lamborghini!

Maybe there was something else on in the same building, she hoped nervously, thinking it was just as well she'd caught a cab. Imagine driving up in her truck.

A security guard was at the entrance. 'Your ticket, ma'am?'

'I... Dr Maddock said he'd leave a ticket for me at the entrance.'

'You're Miss Mardie Rainey?'

'Yes.' *Aargh.* Was it too late to cut and run?

It *was* too late. The man took her arm. 'Take over, Pete,' he called to his colleague. 'Miss Rainey's arrived.'

Had she decided against coming?

The head table needed to sit first. Guests of honour were seated before the riff-raff—if you could call two-thousand-dollar-a-head ticket holders riff-raff.

Regardless, Blake was being ushered to his seat and Mardie wasn't here yet.

'Sir...'

He turned and the security guard was guiding her forward. Mardie.

But different.

She took his breath away.

He thought suddenly of the night years ago, of the premiere of the James Bond movie in Whale Cove. Etta had made Mardie a dress they both thought was the last word in sophistication.

This, though...

Every woman in the room was gowned in sophisticated

splendour. Gowns that clung, satin, silks, sleek this-year's fashion.

Not Mardie. She was dressed…as Mardie.

Her dress did cling. And yes, maybe it was silk, but that was where the comparison ended.

It was tiny, deceptively simple, and it was breathtakingly lovely.

It was a sheath of shimmering fabric that resembled nothing so much as a jewel box straight from the Ottoman Empire. Crimsons, purples, deep pinks, with threads of gold. Simple yet exquisite. It fitted her from breasts to just above the knee as if it was a second skin. It was as if she was wearing a perfect jewel.

She wore a dainty filigree choker around her throat, embedded with stones to match the dress. Enamelled? A Mardie Rainey original? He guessed it was.

Her legs were in shimmering silk stockings. Her stilettos made her legs look as if they went on for ever.

Her curls tumbled over her shoulders, arranged with simplicity and a style that made every other woman's hairstyle seem overdone.

She smiled a greeting to him and he realised everyone in the room had stopped talking.

Why would they not, in the face of this smile?

Mardie…all grown up. Not a country mouse at all.

Mardie, grown past him?

'I'm so glad you could come,' he managed, and the politician's wife he'd been speaking to gave a delighted cry.

'It's Mardie Rainey. Oh, my dear, your work's divine. Are you here with Blake?'

'She is,' Blake said promptly, before Mardie could confirm or deny, and he stepped forward and took her hand.

'Hi,' he said and smiled. He felt like keeping on smiling. Not letting go of her hand.

'Quiet corner?' she said.

'Top table's the quietest.'

'You didn't…'

'I hate going to these functions as a singleton. It messes with the seating plan. The organisers were relieved.'

'Blake…'

'So you've saved the day. Where did you get that dress?'

'I made it.'

Of course. His breath was taken away all over again.

And…these people knew her?

The politician's wife did, at least. 'I've been trying to have Mardie make me some jewellery,' she said. 'Like the choker… Oh, my dear, it's to die for.'

'I'm caught up at the moment,' Mardie said.

'With the memorial wall for the pilot tragedy,' the woman said. 'Yes, but it won't make you money. I'm prepared to pay…'

Mardie smiled politely, made some air promises, turned once again to look at the two empty seats at the top table.

'They're waiting for us,' Blake said.

'I can't believe you did this.'

'You don't enjoy sitting between the gov…'

'No. Don't tell me who they are; I don't want to know,' she said. 'The only way to survive this is to spend dinner telling myself everyone's ordinary.'

He smiled, ushering her to her place. His hand touched the small of her back as she sat. It felt… It felt…

'Blake?'

'Mmm?'

'Remember that time I let you try my bath-boat on the dam?'

'I… Yes.' He did remember.

Back to being eight years old. A wide dam in the back paddock. An ancient bathtub.

Mardie's method of getting from one side of the dam to the other was to seal the bath's open plughole with clay and paddle like crazy. She'd offered to let him try. She hadn't actually told him that the clay plug disintegrated and time was of the essence.

He therefore paddled to the middle and paused to see if there were tadpoles.

The next moment he was neck-deep in tadpoles.

Her lips twitched as she watched him. 'You can remember,' she said.

'I might just…'

'I'm just thinking,' she said, softly but surely. 'Top table, huh? Is this revenge? I'm thinking there has to be an even better fate for you than tadpoles.'

She ate a magnificent dinner, feeling more than a little overwhelmed. Feeling a bit…as if she was pleased she'd dressed up. Initially she'd gone for simple, but when she'd emerged from the bedroom Irena had sent her straight back to change.

'You go anywhere near a guy like that wearing a little black dress, you're out of your mind. You have clothes that could knock his socks off.'

'I don't want to knock his socks off.'

'Then there'll be other women who do,' Irena said bluntly. 'Would you be happy to see him head off into the night with someone else?'

Of course she would. She had no claim on him.

But she'd changed anyway, and she didn't regret it.

She was being treated as Blake's partner. He didn't have time to spend with her. Most of his attention was taken by the Very Important Persons on the far side of him. But every now and then he glanced at her, their eyes met, and it was enough.

He was still Blake. Her friend.

The guy she'd dressed up for.

The people around her—politicians, celebrities—were making small talk. Inanities.

Boring.

So… So why not help? Blake was here for a purpose, she thought suddenly, and she'd been given a free ticket. So why not work the room as Blake was doing?

'I've come to Sydney this week to have my dog's eyes operated on,' she told the guy beside her, slipping the words neatly into a pause in the conversation. 'Cataracts. It's the most marvellous operation. My collie will be back to herding sheep, running on the farm, doing all the things she loves. It's such an amazing operation. And did you know how little it costs in Africa, for a person? Compared to here, it's tiny.' She'd read this on the foundations's website. She knew her facts.

'How awesome would it be?' she said softly. 'To make a blind person see? To give the gift of sight…? How great must it feel to be able to give that gift?'

She sensed, rather than saw, Blake's body stiffen beside her. Whatever he'd been expecting, it hadn't been her taking up the cause.

But she was getting little response. The people around her were hardened to appeals.

The politician's wife was still looking at her choker with longing.

Okay, go sideways. Ignore Blake's stiffening. Do what seems right.

She thought of the pictures of Blake in Africa. The work that could be done…

'My next piece of jewellery…' she said, thinking out loud, eyeing the wife of the Very Important Politician, 'is a choker like this one. If I sell it, I'm thinking that might raise enough for thirty eye-operations. Or more.'

'I'd buy it,' the woman said. 'In a heartbeat.'

'I'll pay more,' the woman opposite said.

'Raffle it,' her partner said, looking amused.

'You'd get more if you auctioned it,' another man said. 'If you're serious?'

'I... Yes.' And she discovered she was.

'How long would it take you to make one?' the politician asked, pushing inexorably forward. 'My wife's been looking at it since you walked in. If I covered the basic cost...'

'I'm donating it,' Mardie said.

Conversation at the far end of the table had stopped. Blake put a hand on her arm. A warning? 'Mardie...'

'I know what I'm doing,' she said. She returned to the politician doing the dealing. 'I need to complete a project I'm working on, but I could easily have the choker made by November.'

'Deal,' the guy said. 'Blake, it's time for you to tell us what we need to know. I'm thinking your lady's offer comes afterwards.'

'Knock 'em dead,' Mardie said and managed to give Blake a smile.

This was what she'd come for. *Tell me about Africa.*

The people around her faded to nothing. She wanted to know.

He'd never been much of a public speaker at school. Was he nervous?

She was nervous on his behalf.

He smiled back at her. Then he touched the choker lightly, a feather touch, and his finger just grazed her neck. Sending a shiver... 'This is to do it justice,' he said and that was exactly what he did.

And she needn't have worried, for this was a Blake she'd never met before.

He greeted his audience with ease, he made a wry observation about the day's political events which made everyone smile—and then he took them to Africa.

Tell me about Africa.

She'd asked and he'd been curt to the point of rudeness.

But not because he didn't care. Not because he couldn't tell it.

Because it was a part of him?

He had a screen behind him, a half-hour documentary where a cameraman had filmed Blake treating children's eyes.

Sound had been recorded along with sight, and the moment the video started the sound of the wind echoed through the room.

They were working in a makeshift tent under a canopy of half-dead trees. The wind sounded appalling. What had he called it? *Arifi*...

It made her shudder. She could feel it through the flimsy fabric of the children's sparse clothing. She could sense it, blasting sand into those vulnerable eyes.

She watched as Blake and his assistants fought to keep the equipment clean, fought to keep the sand at bay, fought to help.

The people...the kids...the damage... That was all he'd said to her when she'd asked. It was practically all he said here. His words were an aside to what was happening on the screen—simple explanations, nothing more.

The cameraman was focusing on the children's faces, and then closer. To eyes that were so damaged...

Blake's commentary was a word at a time, saying what was necessary. Nothing more.

'This is Afi. She's better now, practically a hundred per cent vision in her left eye. Moswen's not so good. Look at the scarring. We're hoping for funding for complex surgery for her but we're not holding our breath. Here's Tawia. Four years old. We caught her early, but where she lives...the flies... She gets infection after infection...'

She was, she discovered, crying. She groped for a tissue and the politician's wife handed her one. The woman had a handful and was using them herself.

Blake was touching these people—influential, wealthy people who could make a difference.

This was Blake fighting for what he was passionate about.

How could she ever have thought he'd gone to medical school to make money?

The presentation finished. Every person in the room was still in Africa.

Blake cleared his papers from the rostrum. Prepared to step down.

A thought…

There was this one moment before people turned back to their wine, their social conversations, before they returned from where they'd been taken.

She slipped the choker from her neck and pushed it to the man who'd asked if it was for sale.

'Take this,' she said simply. 'I should have thought of it. Auction it now.'

'What are you doing?' Blake demanded.

'What I want to do.'

There was no better time…

If these people left, their world would catch up with them. The dinner itself had raised money. Blake's presentation would raise more. But if she could find an outlet for the distress in the room right now…

'There's more where that came from,' she told Blake. He looked as if he'd protest and she reached out and took his hand. Linked her fingers in his.

'Hush,' she said. 'I want to do this.'

So he hushed. They both hushed, while a small and beautiful choker, of copper and semi-precious stones, maybe three hundred dollars of materials and a week of Mardie's work, was sold for an amount that took her breath away.

For Africa.

'And there's another for the losing bidder in November, if she wants it,' she whispered to the auctioneer as the room applauded. 'The same but different. I'm happy to consult on colour and style.'

Bemused, the auctioneer made the offer and the woman accepted, signing a cheque on the spot.

Leaving Mardie hornswoggled.

She'd just sold jewellery for a sum she could scarcely comprehend.

Only Blake's hand was holding her to earth.

'So...so you think we did all right in the fund-raising department?' she managed.

'We did.'

'You were wonderful.'

'Not as wonderful as you,' he said softly. 'But now... You're minus jewellery. I'm thinking... Mardie, would you be interested in a diamond to take its place?'

'A diamond...?'

'Mardie, you are my very best friend. I can't believe what you've just done. To marry you... It would be my honour.'

Her world stilled. He was...proposing? Where had that come from?

He'd taken her breath away.

He'd taken his own breath away. She met his gaze and realised he was as shocked as she was.

Had he meant to say it?

In this crowded room... *A proposal?*

'I don't think...' she said and then found courage. Also a certain amount of indignation. 'No. I don't need to think. Diamonds aren't my style.'

'Not?'

'Hugh gave me the only diamond I want,' she said and she met his gaze squarely. She glanced down at her left hand and it lay there still, her tiny solitaire.

Her armour against future hurt.

'I'm guessing yours would be bigger,' she said. 'But it would come with strings.'

She took a deep breath. Regrouped. She knew his proposal had been instinctive, a spur-of-the-moment response to current emotion. One of them had to be sensible.

'Blake, you asked me once before to become part of your life. That couldn't happen then and it couldn't happen now. For if you were serious—about giving diamonds—I'd be asking you to give yourself. And I don't think you know how.'

'I didn't mean…'

'I know you didn't mean.' Indignation was great. Indignation helped. 'Forget it.'

And then the world took over. The woman who'd bought the option on the second choker came surging forward, twittering her excitement. People needed to speak to Blake. Chequebooks were coming out. He had to work the room.

They glanced at each other and, by mutual consent, turned back to what was important.

His work. Africa.

The work he was doing was breathtaking.

He'd just asked her to marry him?

Be part of his life?

All or nothing. Just as it had been fifteen years ago.

It was surely a mistake. An aberration. He looked as shocked as she was. She concentrated on staying social, doing some ego-massaging, trying to make those chequebooks produce more.

Wondering how soon she could get away.

Blake was mid-negotiation with the head of a huge airline corporation. Something about transport for children who needed specialist care…

One of the Outback doctors was waiting to talk to him.

She could slip away. She must.

She needed to get back to her dogs. Ground herself.

She rose and slipped to the Ladies, then, instead of returning to the crowded dining venue, she just happened to edge outside.

There was a cab rank just…

'Where do you think you're going?'

Blake. Of course. He had eyes in the back of his head, and he'd always been a mind-reader.

She didn't look back but waited for him to come up to her.

'I'm going home.' She fought to sound commonplace. As if he hadn't just asked…*about marriage*? 'I'm worried. Irena's out for the night and I have two dogs locked in her too-small laundry. I need to give them a run.'

'I'll take you.'

'You're needed here.'

'There's no more to be done,' he told her. 'I've organised to meet people from the Outback Medical Service on Thursday—something about mutual knowledge sharing—but they were pushed for time tonight and couldn't stay. The rest is duelling chequebooks. Tonight was every fund-raiser's dream. One person donates on such a grandiose scale—i.e. for your choker—and no one can be seen to be outdone. Even the corporates. It was brilliant. If you knew how many eyes tonight will save…'

'I'm glad.'

'Then let me take you home.'

'The diamond…' she said tentatively.

Their gazes met. Locked. A silent message. *Don't go there.*

'The diamond was a mistake,' he said firmly, as if it really was. 'Said on the spur of the moment because I thought you were wonderful. I still do think you're wonderful, but of course you have Hugh's.'

'Of course.' Why did that make her feel desolate?

Because that was all it was. A diamond with no Hugh behind it.

Nothing.

'So can I take you home?'

'Yes,' she said, and she should have thought of Hugh—but she didn't.

CHAPTER EIGHT

ONCE again they drove to Coogee in near silence. There were so many words between them, but there seemed nothing to say. It was as if there was a chasm between them, with no one courageous enough to step near the edge.

'So you decided against another Mercedes?' she asked, thinking at least his choice of car was a safe enough topic for discussion.

'Do you know how much insurance premiums go up if you crash a Mercedes?' He shrugged. 'It was hired. I decided it was cheaper to buy this time.'

'And you're not a man who wastes money.'

'Are you criticising my choice in cars?'

'Who, me?'

But maybe she was. The car he'd ushered her into was an ancient model, a bit rusty, almost as old as she was.

She glanced across at the man beside her, looking absurdly handsome in yet another dinner suit. How many men had a spare dinner suit?

And drove a Mercedes, followed by a rust bucket.

And looked cool in all of them.

A man of parts.

'So you see this as a long-term investment?' she said cautiously and got a ghost of a smile in return.

'Not too long-term. I'm probably leaving Australia in four weeks.'

'Where will you go?'

'I'm thinking back to California.'

'Back?'

'That's where we used to live,' he said. 'All those years ago. My grandfather set up a charitable trust there. That's what I've expanded—the foundation. Our CEO quit last month. Given…my limitations, it seems sensible that I take on his role.'

She frowned. 'I thought you were the CEO.'

'I'm chairman, because of the family connection. Administration's never been my forte. I far prefer working in the field. I've done the occasional fund-raiser, like this one, but mostly I've left the administration to others. It'll be a good fit for me now, though.'

'Now that you can't do fieldwork?'

'Yes.' Short. Harsh. Desolate.

'You sound like Bessie,' she said softly. 'Charlie said it'd be kinder to put her down if she can't work. Is that how you feel?'

'That's melodramatic.'

'Not so melodramatic if you love your work. Like me if you took the art out of me.'

'It means so much to you?'

'I suspect not as much as your work.'

'So if you were to think of coming to California with me…?' But he said it tentatively, as if he already knew it was out of the question. As they both knew it was.

'That'd be two of us miserable,' she said. 'Why are you asking? For the same reason you asked fifteen years ago? Because you wouldn't mind a security blanket?'

'I would never think of you as a security blanket,' he said vehemently. 'What you did tonight…'

'Was fabulous,' she said, deciding—with a fairly major effort—that she needed to cheer up. Or at least sound as if she'd cheered up. 'It pays to be different. All those diamonds, all those floor-length gowns, and I walk in wearing a home-made tube and costume jewellery. I sit next to the most gorgeous guy in the room and suddenly I'm cool and my choker's desirable and the whole room wants what I'm having. But the money it produced… Can you believe it? How much money do those guys have to play with?'

'You needn't worry,' Blake said. 'Those cheques will be lodged as tax deductions, used to gain all sorts of corporate advantage. The chokers themselves are just icing on the cake. They're not as important as image.'

'That's put me in my place.'

'It was a very nice tax deduction,' he said kindly.

'Oh, the praise. I'm all a-flutter.'

He grinned and suddenly the atmosphere in the car lightened. The stupid issue of diamonds receded. 'It was more than the choker,' he said softly. 'If you knew how much of a difference your actions made…'

'To the kids in Africa?'

'Of course.'

'Do you ever think of anything else?' she ventured.

'It's what I do. It's what I am.'

'Because of Robbie?'

'I don't know any more,' he said simply. 'Yes, when I started it was about Robbie. Now, I love what I do. I believe in it and I'll keep working towards it.'

'So no holidays?'

'Not so much,' he admitted.

'You know,' she said softly, 'maybe you should take some time off before you take on this very important job you have in California. Cut yourself some slack.'

'I don't need slack.'

'You don't do slack. That doesn't say you don't need it. Your face says you haven't done slack in a very long time.'

'I haven't relaxed,' he admitted. Hesitated again. Re-grouped. 'So you'd never think about coming to California?'

'Why would I?'

'We could do good.'

'No,' she said. 'We wouldn't. We'd self-destruct. This is a dumb conversation, Blake. It's unsettling. Leave it. Once upon a time we were friends. Now we have a dog in common and nothing else. We both know it can't ever be any more than that so we might as well stop now.'

Irena was out, at the opening of an art exhibition. 'Don't wait up for me,' she'd told Mardie. 'These things can stretch out for days. Mind, if you get caught up, too…' She'd eyed Mardie thoughtfully. 'Which I hope you do. If my neighbour doesn't see my car, she'll come in and feed the cats. Shall I leave a note saying feed the dogs as well?'

'No!' Mardie had said, revolted, so here she was, back home at eleven at night, not even pumpkin hour. Home to her dogs and Irena's cats.

So much for Irena's hope. Blake hadn't even as much as suggested he'd like to…she didn't know…have crazy, hot sex? Anything.

He'd simply asked her to marry him.

Which was much easier to refuse.

Blake was standing on the doorstep with her. 'I don't like you going into an empty house,' he'd said curtly as she'd told him there was no need. 'And I need to check the dogs are okay.'

The dogs were okay. She opened the door and they prac-tically knocked her over in their joy. Bouncing with excite-ment.

The cats were a picture of smouldering resentment, perched precariously on the curtain rails.

Uh-oh.

It seemed the laundry door hadn't closed properly. She gazed around in dismay at the chaos.

That lamp looked...expensive.

'You'll have to make another choker fast, to pay for this,' Blake said, his lips twitching, and she found herself chuckling.

What was it with this man? He drove her nuts. He was driven by demons she could never hope to compete with, yet underneath...

Underneath he was still just Blake. A boy she'd loved.

A man she could still love?

Should she take his proposal seriously?

Maybe he had been serious, she thought. He wasn't a man who took things lightly.

He'd asked because he meant it?

If he had...

If he had, there was part of her that ached to accept. Only of course it hadn't been a proper proposal. It was just like that invitation to come with him to university all those years ago. Come to California. All or nothing. Be subsumed by his life.

Share his demons?

She had no intention of sharing his demons. No way. She had enough of her own.

He was helping her fight down the over-excited dogs. He was too near.

How to tell him to go home?

How to tell him he was far too distracting?

'I...I need to change and take the dogs for a walk,' she said. 'I need to get rid of some energy.'

'You're not walking in the dark.'

'It's Coogee,' she said patiently. 'It'll be lit like daylight. Security patrols. The works. I've done it before. The security guys even know me—at this time of night they'll turn a blind eye if I let Bounce off his lead.'

'How often do you come down here?'

'I sell my enamelling,' she said patiently. 'I live in two worlds.'

'So you could come to California…'

'No, Blake, I couldn't,' she snapped. 'Have you forgotten my mother? Have you forgotten how much I love Banksia Bay? And have you even begun to realise how much I don't know you? Enough. You're welcome to come for a walk on the beach with me, but that's the extent of it. If you have time to wait until I put some jeans on. If you don't mind walking in a dinner suit.'

'Lately I've been doing all sorts of strange things in a dinner suit,' he said, sounding grim.

'Maybe your life's changing in more ways than one,' she said. 'Think about it. California doesn't sound like much fun to me. How about some lateral thinking?'

As if… When had this man ever changed direction? Was it possible that he ever could?

He stood and waited until she put on jeans and windcheater and trainers, and when she came back to the sitting room he couldn't figure whether he loved her more in her wonderful home-made dress or in her casual jeans.

Love…

It was a simple word but it was resounding more and more.

Mardie.

Mardie herding sheep. Mardie tackling the tree with her chainsaw.

Mardie loving her mother, loving her community.

Love.

But he didn't truly know what love was and how he was feeling now… He didn't know what to do with it. There was nowhere to take it.

He'd asked her to marry him. What if she'd said yes?

He'd make it work.

She wasn't taking the risk. She was being wise for both of them.

Beach, walk, dogs.

He tossed his jacket and tie, rolled up his sleeves, pretended to be casual.

Pretended he could fit into Mardie's world.

He knew that he couldn't.

He'd expected a stroll. He didn't get one. Mardie walked as if there was a sheep in trouble down the back paddock and she wasn't wasting time getting there.

The tide was far out. The foreshore was well lit but even if it hadn't been, the full moon made walking a pleasure. They could walk for miles on the ribbon of wet sand and on the paths around the cliffs—and maybe she intended just that. She was striding as if she meant to leave him behind.

That was okay. It felt okay that she was simply on the beach beside him.

More—it felt good.

It felt good to the dogs, too. Strange smells. Shallows to run in. Humans to herd. Both these dogs must know the sea. Bessie stuck to Bounce's side, but she seemed almost the leader, egging Bounce on.

Blake let his attention stay on the dogs. It was easier to think dogs rather than think Mardie, for every time he thought about Mardie…

Mardie tonight, glowing, sophisticated, beautiful, generous. Every man in the room watching her. His Mardie-girl…

To walk away…

Not his.

Don't think about it.

Think of Bessie.

To cure her would give such pleasure. It wouldn't feel so bad going back to California knowing he'd left Mardie with two dogs instead of one.

Why had he asked her to marry him?

He hadn't been serious. If he seriously wanted this woman to marry him, he needed to get down on bended knee and do the thing in style.

The answer would be the same. The idea was, as she'd said, unworkable.

Unthinkable.

Except he was thinking it.

Marriage on his terms?

Marriage for him; not for Mardie.

Bad idea.

'So what were you about, offering diamonds?' Mardie asked, still striding, and he wondered if she was angry. She'd never been one to sulk in silence. Bring the elephant into the room and inspect it from all angles.

'Thinking aloud,' he said. 'Wishing our worlds could collide.'

'Would you really want our worlds to collide?' she asked. 'Or is it more that in your world you don't have anything of my world? And my world feels safe.'

'Safe...'

'Why did you come back to Australia after your illness?' she asked. 'I know there was this fund-raiser, but someone else could surely have handled it. If home's in California...'

'It's not.'

'Home has to feel somewhere.'

She slowed. She'd kicked off her sandals and was walking in the shallows.

He'd been walking a little up the beach where it was drier. As she slowed he tugged off his shoes and hit the water, too. Her anger seemed to have dissipated. He flinched as the first wave hit and she smiled.

That smile... Marriage... Why wouldn't a man ask, even if the concept was impossible?

The dogs came tearing back to them, crazy circling, as if making sure their flock of humans stayed in a tight knot.

He wouldn't mind staying in a tight knot with Mardie.

Home was…

Here. With this woman.

It always had been. Ever since that first day in the playground. Sharing lunches.

Why had he come back to Australia?

It had been his refuge after Robbie died. He'd found peace here. He still thought of Australia as a refuge.

He couldn't stay somewhere because it was a refuge. He couldn't love somewhere because it was safe.

He couldn't love a woman for the same reasons.

Mardie was much, much more.

'Ooh, there's some stuff going on in that head of yours,' she said. 'For heaven's sake, Blake, let it go. Race you back to the headland. You could always beat me, but you've been sick and I've been training. One, two, three, go…'

And she was off, flying along the wet sand, her dogs hurtling along behind her. Dogs and woman…

He'd never met someone so…free.

She had her demons. Of course she did.

She chose to let them take care of themselves.

Maybe he, too…

No. Too hard. It was far too hard.

She beat him—of course she did—he'd spent the first half of the race in stupid, unproductive thought—and when he did finally catch her, she seemed angry again. They were at the start of the path up to the house. She didn't pause; she went right on up, and when they reached his car parked out the front, she fussed over dog leads and didn't look at him.

He waited until she straightened. Tried to figure what to say.

She held out her hand. A formal gesture of farewell.

'I've had a lovely night,' she said, a trifle too stiffly. 'Thank you.'

'That's… I've enjoyed it, too.'

'I can manage on my own now, with the dogs.'

'I'll be here on Thursday when Colin operates.'

'There's no need.'

'I'll be here.'

'Thank you,' she said simply. 'That would be lovely. Goodnight.'

And before he could react, before he could reach out a hand and take hers—she slipped into the house with her dogs without another word.

Tuesday and Wednesday, he didn't see her. There was no reason.

She needed to take Bessie back to the vet's for a couple more pre-op tests, but she lived close and for him to take the half-hour trip there…

As she'd said, there was no need.

He had things to do. There were always things to do.

One of the cheques for Mardie's chokers bounced. He was used to that. Guys big-noting themselves among their peers, then letting the charity cope with the consequences.

He made a few enquiries, discovered the guy did have serious money, discovered he'd tried this on before.

He made a couple of calls to the media, had a journalist do a dig story and he had a phone call from the bank within the hour.

The cheque had magically been cleared.

There was no way the scum-bag was getting Mardie's choker without paying.

He could do good, he thought, as he tallied the figures for Monday night. He could make the foundation much bigger than it was now. He could make it huge.

He wanted to work in the field.

But that was dumb. The cause was what counted. To die of dengue because he wanted to be indispensable… How would Robbie feel about that?

His twin. The guy who questioned everything he did.

How would Robbie feel about Mardie?

There was a dumb question. A dumb thought.

Put her out of his mind.

Then suddenly he thought…Irena. Irena was Mardie's agent. If Mardie had an agent then there must be more sales.

Mardie had looked him up. He could do the same. He did an internet search for one Mardie Rainey, looking for stockists. Discovered a tiny gallery that specialised in three-dimensional art.

He just happened to walk past. He just happened to walk in, expecting rings, bracelets, maybe even chokers like he'd seen on Monday night.

Instead he found tiny enamelled pictures. This then, was how she'd landed the job commemorating the pilots. Where she'd gained her reputation.

These pictures were extraordinary.

They were of…nothing. Glass on copper.

A blade of grass against a weathered fence post.

A piece of driftwood on a beach.

A raindrop.

Nothing.

Everything.

He looked at them and thought of Africa. A child's sight.

So little. Everything.

He thought of Mardie's life.

And he thought of his own.

Thursday. 'Have her here at eight. No breakfast,' Colin had decreed and Mardie had Bessie there at seven forty-five. She stayed in the truck until the clinic doors opened, hugging Bessie, wishing they'd elected to have only one eye done today and not both. Both eyes seemed scary.

Even one seemed scary.

She'd left Bounce with Irena and the cats. Bessie had to do this alone.

She had to do this alone.

Bessie seemed bereft, and she felt exactly the same.

But then... Her truck door swung open and Blake was there. Just...there.

Deep breath. This was good. Wasn't it? Two of them could feel bad about Bessie together.

He was so close.

He'd asked her to marry him. The question had hovered in her head for two days.

Stupid.

She was so happy to see him again she could hardly speak.

'S...so tell me again why we're doing both eyes?' she managed.

'So we won't have to spend another night like last one,' he said. 'Staring into the dark thinking of all the things that can go wrong.'

'You, too?'

'I know the odds,' he said. 'Healthy dog, healthy eyes under the cataracts, great surgeon, tried-and-tested procedure—this is as good as it gets. The biggest risk is retina detachment and that's a risk no matter whether we do one or both. It'll be fine.'

'Yet you still sat up all night.'

'Yep,' he said and lifted Bessie from her arms. 'I'm a sucker for a lady with facial hair. Colin's here. All systems go. Let's get our Bessie's sight restored so she can get on with her life.'

'Blake?'

'Mmm.'

'Did you come…just to wish us luck?'

'I'll stay close until it's done. I've agreed to meet a couple of guys at the airport in an hour but that's close enough to here. If you'd like me to stick around…'

'I would.' She hesitated. She shouldn't need this man.

'I definitely would,' she said.

They stayed with Bessie until the anaesthetic took hold, but then they had to leave.

'You're not watching,' Colin told him. 'Blake taught me,' he explained to Mardie. 'If there's anything guaranteed to make my hands shake, it's my teacher watching. Take him away and don't let him come near until I've finished.'

'Fine by me,' Mardie said, feeling bad. She hugged Bessie and left. Feeling…watery.

She pushed open the door to outside with more force than necessary.

Blake ushered her through. Closed the door after her. Offered her a tissue.

Went a step further and hugged her.

'I don't cry,' she managed. Not pulling away.

'You shouldn't. Bessie's about to be cured. What's there to cry about?'

'Do you get emotional about patients?'

'Never.'

'Liar.' She knew this guy.

'I shouldn't.'

She sniffed. She managed—with a pretty big effort—to pull herself out of his arms. Blew her nose, hard.

Got a grip.

'So you want me to stay here while you have your meeting at the airport?'

'Stay with me,' he said softly and took her hand.

She gazed down at their linked hands.

Thought, inexplicably, of Bessie and Bounce. Practically Siamese twins.

She didn't pull away.

What was he doing, meeting these guys? He was wasting time.

He'd met them the night of the dinner. Riley and Harry. Doctor and pilot with an Outback Flying Doctor medical service based at Whale Cove. Squeezing the dinner in between care flights.

It seemed Harry was a friend of Raff's, the Banksia Bay cop. Raff had told them about him. They'd come on Monday night to listen. Asked if they could talk to him.

A job offer? Questions about fund-raising? Normally he'd decline but he'd been feeling…disoriented. As if he didn't know how to say no.

Now…he and Mardie watched as the light plane came in to land, a patient was transferred to an ambulance headed for a city hospital, and then Harry and Riley were free.

They didn't speak. They simply waited.

With their patient transferred, the men came over to them. Big men, tough, in the uniform of the Flying Doctor Service.

'Raff says you're looking for a job,' Riley said bluntly, straight to the point.

Raff. Banksia Bay. Of course. Everyone knew everyone.

'He has his wires crossed. I'm not.'

But it seemed Raff had done some research. He'd worked fast and he had it right. 'Raff says you've been in Africa treating eyes,' Riley said. 'He says you can't go back because of dengue. Now he thinks you're planning to be a pen-pusher. That'd be just plain dumb. We could use you, right here, right now. There's no dengue where we work, just a whole heap of need.'

* * *

It wouldn't work.

They drove back to the vet clinic and the silence in the truck was almost tangible.

Blake was staring straight ahead.

'I'm going back to California,' he said at last. 'I think I have to.'

'So you met them why?'

'I thought they might want to talk mutual fund-raising.' But he hadn't. He'd known the minute he'd met them that there was a job on the line. If he and Mardie…

No.

'You wouldn't consider it?' she ventured. 'Robbie doesn't give you that option?'

'I should never have told you about Robbie.' It was an explosion.

'I should have guessed.' She hesitated, and then went on. 'Blake, that night, all those years ago,' she said softly. 'I can only imagine. Two little boys, lying in that great big house. Following rules. But then…the joy of sneaking out to play in the pool. Two little boys having fun. And tragedy. But surely that doesn't mean you need to follow rules all your life, especially if those rules are ones you've set up for yourself. If those rules were meant to make up for Robbie, they never can. They never will.'

'This is…'

'None of my business? Maybe not. Or maybe it is my business, because you're my friend.' She took a deep breath. 'On Monday you even suggested I marry you. It was offhand, like something I wouldn't even consider, but you know something? I would.'

'Mardie…'

'Only not with your shadows,' she said, with only the faintest tremor behind the words. 'For I'm not sharing.' Another deep breath. 'Blake, have you ever talked to seven-year-old Blake?'

'What do you mean?'

'It's a thing you do,' she said diffidently. 'It's a thing I learned. When Hugh died...I was a mess and our local doctor organised a shrink to see me. You know what was going round my head? That I hadn't put the dogs in their crate. I'd cleaned it and then we were running late so I thought—why bother putting it back? So they were fussing in the back seat, and Hugh was telling them to pipe down, and the kids came round the bend. He didn't have time to swerve. If he'd had that extra split second... I thought... Well, you know what I thought.'

'It wasn't your fault.'

'Yeah, you say that. Everyone says it but you can hear it as many times as you want and not believe. You know that better than me. But the shrink... You know what he did? He made me find a picture of me from before the accident. And he said I needed to treat the hurting me as separate. The Mardie-Before and the Mardie-After. And the Mardie-After needed to talk to the Mardie-Before, talk through exactly what happened that day, tell her that what she did wasn't criminal or even stupid. He said I should give that Mardie a hug and move on. And you know what? Eventually I did.'

He didn't say anything. Nothing.

'So...could you look at a photograph of your seven-year-old self, and tell him he has to pay for the rest of his life?' she ventured. 'Or would you look at that seven-year-old and give him a hug and weep for what he's gone through already? Robbie's death. Your parents' abandonment. And then...could you tell the little boy that you were to live his life as he ought to live his life? To have fun. To do good if that's what you want, but only if that's what you want, not because you're paying back shadows. To...' She paused. Thought about it. Finally said it. 'To allow yourself to be happy.'

'I think we should leave it,' he said heavily, and she thought, yes, she should. She'd said everything she could say.

Or...not quite.

Just say it.

'And, as for Monday... As for the diamond...I would marry you,' she said simply. 'In truth, I decided when I was ten that I wanted to marry you. And it seems I've never stopped. I loved Hugh, but in a different way; he was a different man. It doesn't take away what I felt for him, what I feel for you. It seems I've loved you all the time and I guess I always will. Shadows or not. But if you can't get rid of your shadows I guess our loving will keep us at a distance. Because there's no choice. For both of us.'

They met a beaming Colin.

'I couldn't ask for better,' he said. 'Textbook perfect. It's gone brilliantly in both eyes. She's on the way to recovery. All she needs is absolute quiet, to wear the cone collar all the time, no barking, drops twice a day, total care, and in four weeks I'm thinking you'll have a magnificent working dog. Do you want to see her? She's still heavily sedated.'

They went in and saw her.

Her eyes were still closed. Colin gently lifted a lid and the awful milkiness was gone.

Mardie felt... She felt...

Good. Excellent. Dog-wise, at least, this was job done. She could get on with her life with two dogs.

Blake would go back to the US. Things would return to normal.

But, despite her tumultuous emotions, Colin's words were starting to sink in. Quiet. Cone collar. No barking. Total care...

She didn't quite have a handle on this.

'No barking at all?' she said, faltering.

'I thought Blake would have explained post-op care,' Colin said, frowning.

'Blake did mention it,' she said. 'I just thought... I can

handle eye drops.' She took a deep breath. 'No. Sorry. I can handle everything. I'll take Bounce to the boarding kennels for a month. It won't kill him. If Bessie's locked inside, she'll stay quiet.'

'You're hardly ever inside.' Blake said.

'I guess loneliness is the price she pays for her sight.'

'It's not,' Blake said.

'Not?'

'I have an apartment here in the city,' he said. 'I'll be working here for the next few weeks. I do some online teaching,' he explained as they both looked at him in surprise. 'I can do that while I keep Bessie at my feet. I know she'll miss Bounce but it'll work. I'll bring her back to the farm in a month, just before I go.'

There was the solution, just like that. Easy.

Mardie looked down at the sleeping dog. Bessie.

It should feel great.

It was an eminently practical solution.

She could walk away. Go back to Irena's, collect Bounce, go back to the farm.

Blake would return Bessie to her in a month. And then... nothing.

It was a neat solution all round.

It felt...

It felt...

Not neat.

'That's great,' she said, sounding feeble. 'I... You have your car here, Blake? I can go, then. I really would like to get back to the farm this afternoon.' She put her hand on Bessie's soft head, taking as well as giving comfort.

'Take care of her,' she whispered. 'Thank you, Colin. And...and thank you, Blake. You're both wonderful.'

'I'm not wonderful,' Blake said.

'Yes, you are,' she said, gaining strength. 'Yes, you are, if you let yourself be.'

CHAPTER NINE

FOUR weeks was a very long time in the life of Mardie.

She did exactly what she'd been doing a month ago. She spent three days a week in the nursing home, helping aged fingers give pleasure to their owners, having fun. She worked furiously on her last plates, and then slowed because Robyn Partling's life refused to be told in a rush. In a month they were done and she loved them.

She could take them to Sydney this weekend and deliver them.

Or not.

This weekend Blake had said he'd bring Bessie home, and something inside her—the silly, hormonal something—was saying, *Last chance, Last chance, Last chance.*

He rang, friendly but curt. 'She's done brilliantly,' he told her. 'Colin's taken the cone off. Her eyesight's amazing. He says she's ready for farm life again. Can you be home at two on Saturday?'

'Of course,' she said simply—and then she was nervous. Really nervous.

What was she doing, thinking *last chance*? There never was going to be a chance. He'd drop off Bessie and say good-bye and fly out to California and that'd be the end of an unsettling period of her life.

She had to settle.

Which meant…normal.

Saturday.

She went to see Charlie and told him Bessie's latest news. She told her mum.

'We'd love to see her come home,' they both said, and she thought—normal; I can do that.

Two o'clock on Saturday.

Blake was coming home.

No. Bessie was coming home. Blake was merely the delivery man.

He turned into the farm gate, expecting the old Mardie. Mardie in her jeans and an ancient sweater—the Mardie who belonged here, not the unsettling Mardie who'd blown him away in Sydney.

He wanted it to be the old Mardie. He'd take the thought of her back to the States with him, he thought, as he'd carried her in his thoughts for years. She was a warm part of his heart that had stayed safe, that was used for comfort but not permitted to interfere with what he had to do.

He wanted that part of him to stay unaltered.

He looked to the veranda and there she was, on the top step, Bounce beside her.

Bessie was harnessed in the back seat but he heard her whine.

'Home,' he told her and the word felt…

Yeah, like the word he wasn't allowed to feel. He needed to hand Bessie over and get out of here, memories intact.

He pulled up. Bounce tore down from the veranda, Mardie following a trifle more sedately but not much. She was smiling.

What cost that smile?

'Bessie.' He let her out and Mardie was on her knees, hugging, and Bounce was going wild, trying to reach his friend. He watched the group hug and felt his heart twist.

'Bessie.' It was a quavering voice from the veranda and Bessie froze. Pulled out from the group hug in an instant.

Looked up.

Really looked.

Her eyes worked fine. Her hearing was even better. She knew who was on the veranda and she was gone, flying across the yard, up the steps, reaching the old man in the vast padded hospital chair. Skidding to a stop. Not jumping. Just sitting, hard beside him.

Charlie's gnarled old hand dropped to her silky head and she quivered from nose to tail. She put a paw up, as if in entreaty. Quivered some more.

'Up,' he whispered and she needed no more persuasion. She was up on his blanketed knees, licking his face, her paws on his shoulders, doing what an untrained, out-of-control dog would do when reunited with her beloved owner.

Only this was no untrained dog. Charlie chuckled and submitted to licking, and even hugged back himself, but he was frail and he knew it.

'Enough,' he said, and Bessie was off his knee in an instant, sitting beside him, looking adoringly up at him. Charlie was smiling and smiling.

So was Blake.

And Mardie.

And so was her mother, and the nurse who stood silently behind. Groping for tissues all round.

He'd thought he was bringing Bessie back to Mardie. Instead… Here were Charlie and Etta and a nurse with a name tag that said she was Liz, administrator of the Banksia Bay Nursing Home. He was bringing Bessie home to Banksia Bay, to be enveloped once again in this all-embracing town.

'Welcome home,' Mardie said as he reached her, to him alone, and she hugged him unself-consciously, as if it was the most natural thing in the world.

Could he accept that welcome?

He thought suddenly of that night all those years ago, shut in the house, bored, tired, fed up with listening to the grown-up party downstairs. One moment's breaking of the rules. *Let's go out and swim.*

That moment felt like now.

'You want to see what she can do?' Charlie asked, his voice cracked with age and pride, and the moment when he could have hugged Mardie back was past. When he could have whirled her round and round in his arms and held her to him and declared he, too, was truly home…

It was a fantasy. A stupid, dangerous longing.

'Of course,' he managed and put Mardie aside, and heaven alone knew the effort that cost him.

'Charlie's wonderful with dogs,' Etta said placidly from her chair, looking from Mardie to Blake and back again, and Blake knew she was asking questions in her mind that couldn't be answered.

'Charlie's the best dog-trainer in the district,' Liz said. 'Half the dogs in this town have been trained by Charlie, or by guys Charlie's trained to train, and the younger dogs have reached the stage where they seem almost to have been trained by Charlie's dogs. Generations of dogs, teaching each other, courtesy of Charlie. His legacy will live for ever.'

Charlie's wrinkled face worked; he tried not to smile, tried not to look as if he wasn't moved. But he was.

Even in the past four weeks Charlie had slipped; Blake could see that.

Liz was giving him a gift. An affirmation.

As maybe in his turn Charlie had gifted each of them.

Banksia Bay. His refuge. Blake felt…

Mardie took his hand and squeezed, but it was a message, nothing more.

He couldn't feel.

The offer from the Flying Dotor… An insidious siren song. Not as insidious as Mardie.

'I've put some sheep in the home paddock,' she said. 'You want to help take Mum and Charlie down to watch these guys strut their stuff?'

To be drawn further into this emotion?

He had no choice. There was no escaping, but did he want to escape?

Yes. He told himself that harshly.

Only not yet. All eyes were on him. He was their audience. He was Charlie's affirmation.

So they took the two big hospital chairs across to the gate into the home paddock where Mardie had herded six sheep. They were young ones, yearlings, wild and silly, ready to run any which way.

She'd set pegs up at intervals and a tiny corral in the centre of the paddock, with an entrance about the width of a man. Or a sheep.

'Walk up,' Charlie said to Bessie and Bessie's eyes, the eyes that had been hidden for so long, lit with excitement and pure instinctive pleasure.

'Stay,' Mardie told Bounce and Bounce quivered and stayed.

'In here,' Charlie said, his voice scarcely a whisper, but Bessie heard. 'Look back. Get back, take time, come by...'

And in moments the sheep were transformed from a bunch of silly youngsters to a beautifully controlled, collie-trained flock. Bessie moved almost without command, glancing back at Charlie every so often, a tiny glance, watching Charlie's hand. Watching each and every one of the sheep. Weaving them seamlessly through the pegs, out and back, out and back, and then into the tiny gap and into the makeshift coral.

Done.

As a display of sheer skill, of communication between man and dog, it was breathtaking.

'That'll do,' Charlie said gruffly and Bessie came flying

back to his side and sat again, totally attentive, waiting for the next order.

'He's… Charlie's been teaching me,' Mardie said in a voice that was none too steady. 'Want to watch?'

So they watched as Bounce gave it his best.

He wasn't close to as slick as Bessie was. The communication between Bounce and Mardie wasn't as great. At one stage he saw Bessie half stand, as if aching to help. Charlie's hand rested on her head.

'Stay,' he said softly. 'Young 'uns have to learn.'

And Bounce was learning and so was Mardie. The sheep were eventually back in the corral and Mardie's beam was as wide as a house.

'How's that?'

'They all clapped and laughed and Bounce bounced back to Bessie. Charlie released her, and the dogs did a wide joyous circle of the whole paddock. Not touching. There was no longer need for touch. Bessie had her eyes back. Still they didn't leave each other. Siamese twins. Touching at the heart.

Mardie's hand was suddenly in his, and this time there was no pressure. No message. It was simply because…she wanted her hand to be in his.

'Thank you,' she said softly. 'Thank you from all of us.'

He wanted to kiss her.

He wanted to kiss her more than anything else in the world.

Robbie… Don't go near the pool…

Mardie deserved more than being used as a refuge.

'I need to go,' he said and glanced at his watch. 'I… There's things to do. I leave for the States on Tuesday.'

'Of course.' She tugged back, reminded of reality. 'You can't stay for…'

'No.' Blunt. Curt. He watched Etta's face fall.

He didn't see Mardie's face fall. He carefully wasn't looking at Mardie. He'd pulled right away.

'I'll walk you to your car,' she said.

'I'll put the kettle on,' Liz said. 'You guys play with the dogs for a few more minutes,' she told Charlie and Etta. 'Mardie and I'll push you inside when the kettle boils.'

Liz had thus given them privacy. It meant Mardie could walk him back to the car and they didn't have an audience,

Mardie slipped her hand back into his as they walked.

He should pull away. He didn't.

'I'm sad you're going back,' she said softly. 'You could have made a difference with North Coast Rescue.'

'I'll make a difference with what I'm doing.'

'By sitting in an office?'

'I'm good at fund-raising.'

'Yes, but does it give you pleasure?'

'That's not the point.'

'No.' She pulled her hand away.

They reached the car. He should get in and go. Leave. Drive away and never come back.

'I should never have come,' he said.

'I'm glad you did. It's like…closure.'

'I've always hated that word.'

'Me, too,' she whispered and she turned into him. Looked up.

And he didn't get into the car.

For first there was something he had to do. Something he had no choice in, for every nerve in his body was telling him to do it.

He cupped her chin with his hands, he stooped and he kissed her.

Her lips met his. Merged.

Heat, want, need. It exploded between them, surging at the point of contact and spreading.

It was as if his world had suddenly melted, merged, fused. All centring round this one point.

This woman in his arms.

He held her, gently and then more urgently. She was on tip-toe to meet him and he lifted her, hugging her close. Melting.

Mardie. His Mardie.

Not his Mardie. He'd made his decision.

But to walk away would hurt. Why not savour this last piece of surrender, for surrender it surely was? Surrendering himself to what he wanted most in the world.

This woman in his arms.

This woman he was kissing.

This woman who was kissing him. For the roles were changing, the delineation was blurring.

A man and a woman and a need as primeval as time itself.

History was disappearing. History and pain and even sense. Especially sense.

His defences were crumbling as he held her, as her breasts crushed against his chest, as she merged into him.

Mardie.

He'd met her when he was too young to know what a woman was. She'd become part of him in a slow, insidious process that now seemed inevitable, unalterable. She was like part of him, part of his childhood, part of his teens, but...part of who he was right now.

She knew him as no other woman could know him. She'd exposed parts of him he'd hidden with years of carefully built barriers, because behind the barriers...pain.

Where was the pain now?

Not here. Not with this kiss. Not with this wonder.

It was waiting. He knew that, even as he surrendered to the here and now, to the pure loveliness of this moment. Self-recriminations were right behind him, waiting to take over. But he had this one moment. His kiss intensified, became more urgent, more compelling.

Mardie...

But she was suddenly withdrawing, just a little. He felt her body stiffen. Her hands fought to find purchase between them, and she pushed him away.

It felt as if part of himself was being torn, to let her go.

He had to let her go.

'This…this is *some* goodbye kiss,' she said in a voice that said she was shaken to the core.

'It is.' He wanted to reach out and touch her again. Gather her back into his arms.

Surrender…

Stay here. Stay safe. Banksia Bay. Mardie. Its own sweet siren song.

Staying safe couldn't last. The world was out there.

To retreat… To come home…

It wasn't his home.

'Thank you…for being you,' he said simply. 'I've loved this time.'

'No, you haven't. It's torn you in two.'

'Maybe it has,' he said simply. 'But at least now, when I walk away I know there's truth between us. Friendship.'

'Like that will help.'

'Mardie…'

'I know,' she said bleakly. 'You can't help it. You need to save the world and somehow you think you can't do it here. You can't think that I do it, that my mum did it, that Liz up there does it, that Charlie does it, too, in his way.' She paused. Closed her eyes. Took a deep breath.

'Sorry. You don't understand and you'll never understand. Off you go and save the world in your own way, my lovely Blake, and know I'll always think of you. With love. Because I can't help myself. But there'll always be a little part of Banksia Bay that's home for you, Blake, whether you want it or not. Don't forget it. Don't forget us.'

* * *

They were waiting for her. Her mother, Charlie, Liz and the two dogs.

Bessie whimpered as if she realised what she'd lost and Charlie hushed her.

Her mother held out her hand and she took it and then stooped and let Etta hug her. Her mother's hugs… Once upon a time they'd made things better. Not now.

'He's not coming back?' Liz asked.

'What do you think?'

'Sorry, girl,' Charlie said.

There was a moment's silence while they all thought of something to say.

Then… 'That dog of yours needs work,' Charlie said roughly. 'You want a quick lesson before Liz orders us all in for scones and tea?'

'Yes, please,' she said, trying valiantly not to…well, not to stand and wail. A girl had some pride.

'Well, let's get on with it,' Charlie said. 'Time's short. We've got things to do. Get yourself together, girl, and move on.'

'You're tired,' Liz said.

'Not too tired for what she loves,' Charlie retorted. 'Never too tired for that.'

He drove back to Sydney feeling empty.

So what was new? He'd had this emptiness in his gut for ever.

Not when he was with Mardie. When he was with Mardie she filled his life.

It was a dangerous, insidious sweetness.

Why couldn't a man just give in?

And do what…?

North Coast Rescue would give him a job in a heartbeat. 'We fly clinics three days a week,' Riley had told him. 'We almost always fly north. It'd be a snap to detour through

Banksia Bay—there's a light airstrip at the back of the town. We could pick you up on the way, drop you off on the way back. Long days, but, mate, they're so satisfying.'

Three days a week. The rest… Writing? Teaching online? Doing some foundation work?

Helping Mardie train Bounce.

He'd never change the world.

He'd change a little bit.

It wasn't enough to stop this fierce, desolate drive within him.

How could he let it go?

See a shrink in the States? Come back cured?

No. He'd come back with the guilt in recess. He could never live with Mardie on those terms—she deserved so much more.

Get over it.

He thought of what he'd left behind. Mardie. Etta and Charlie. Bounce and Bessie. Sheep and hens, beach and farm.

It had been a refuge when he was a child. It had been a refuge now as he came to terms with dengue.

A man couldn't stay in a refuge for ever. He had to face his demons on his own.

He returned to Sydney.

He spent time consulting with two Australian doctors who'd volunteered to spend a year each in Africa.

He packed up the apartment, and put it on the market. It had been stupid to keep it all these years. He was never coming back.

Two more days… The loose ends were being tied.

Monday night. At one in the morning, he was staring at the ceiling, waiting for sleep that wouldn't come.

A phone call.

'Blake?'

Mardie. He was upright in an instant, flicking on the light. Her voice…

'What's happened?'

'No…no drama,' she said but he could tell by her voice that she'd been crying. 'It's just…Charlie died yesterday. In his sleep. It's…it's fine. It was his time. Liz…Liz knew he was slipping. She came out and got Bessie, and Bessie was asleep on his bed when he died. He knew she was there. He knew she was safe, and well and happy.' She caught her breath. Struggled to go on.

'It's just… I wasn't going to tell you, you don't need to know, but then I thought…I couldn't sleep so I thought I'd tell you and you can do what you want with it. His funeral's this afternoon. No one's expecting you to come. It's…it's nothing to do with you but I thought…I thought I'd let you know and let you decide whether it's anything to do with you or not.'

She shouldn't have told him.

She sat in the front pew, with her mother in her wheelchair beside her and Bessie at her feet. The Banksia Bay vicar saw nothing wrong and everything right with Charlie's dog being here, being part of the ceremony.

Charlie's coffin was loaded with every trophy, every ribbon, he and his dogs had ever won. There were photographs everywhere.

Charlie and dogs. He'd never had children but his dogs lived on.

Mardie was almost totally focused on Charlie, almost totally focused on what the vicar was saying. But a tiny part of her was aware of the door.

This one last chance…

He wasn't taking it. He wouldn't come.

'It's okay, sweetheart, you have us,' her mother whispered, taking her hand, and she flushed. Was she so obvious?

'I don't need anyone.'

'Nonsense,' Etta said sharply. 'We all need everyone.'

He came. He'd meant to go in. At the last minute he stopped himself. He still felt as if he had no place here.

Going in would be a statement he had no wish to make.

Instead he parked his car on the hill overlooking the church. Watched people go in. Watched people gather outside. Many, many people, most of them attached to…dogs?

The service was being broadcast on loudspeakers so the crowd outside could hear. The day was still and warm, and the sound carried.

He heard people talk of Charlie, with respect and with affection.

He heard Mardie. Had they asked her to speak the eulogy, then? Her voice came over the loudspeaker, true and clear. 'Charlie's dog, Bessie, is here. If Bessie has a voice, here's what she'd like to say about Charlie…'

Laughter. Murmurs of agreement, of affection, of wistfulness from the congregation.

Old hymns. Favourites he remembered from when Mardie's mum had bossed them into church.

They felt like something he missed. Like part of him, cut off.

And then a blaze of bagpipes, the ancient tune, "Dawning of that Day," signalling the end of the service.

The crowd parted so the pall-bearers could carry their burden out.

But they didn't just part.

They formed a guard of honour, all the way from the church door to the graveyard at the foot of the hill where he stood.

A man or woman or child was suddenly standing every step of the way, on either side of the path where the coffin was carried. And beside each man, woman and child…

A dog. Not just a dog, but a trained dog. Mostly working dogs—collies, kelpies, blue heelers, but the occasional poodle, spaniel, mutt.

Every dog was sitting hard on his owner's heels, rigidly to attention, eyes straight in front as the coffin passed, a last and loving respect to the man who'd spent his life training them. Who'd passed on his skills from dog to dog, from generation to generation.

Mardie was walking behind the coffin. Bessie was beside her, not on a lead, heeling beautifully, steady, sure.

Behind Mardie, others—friends, relatives, more dogs. Liz was pushing Etta's chair. Bounce was heeling by the wheelchair as if he realised the significance of this day.

A community, mourning its own.

He thought suddenly of Mardie's plates. Her skill in creating things of wonder, the pilot's wife's awe and gratitude.

He thought of Etta, Mardie's mother, her crazy cooking, the way she'd welcomed a stray little boy into her home.

He looked at Liz, who ran one of the best nursing homes he'd ever been in.

Of Raff, the local cop, who cared for this community with firmness and with love.

Love…

He thought of the children he'd treated in Africa. All those lives, altered because of what he'd done.

He thought of what he could do…

He could go back to California. Make Eyes For Africa bigger.

Others could do that. Others would do that. He could keep an overseeing role.

He could stay here and make Mardie happy.

She was already happy. She didn't need him.

He should…

No. Enough of *should*.

The procession had reached the graveyard now. Mardie was

standing by the open grave, Bessie by her side. She looked... alone.

Enough.

He walked down the hillside to join her.

Not because he should. Not because it'd save the world.

He walked down to join Mardie because it was what he most wanted to do in the world.

If he could make Mardie love him... If he could be part of this community...the world would be his.

She'd been aware of him for a while, high on the hill, just watching.

He was too far away for her to be sure, but she knew. A sixth sense...

Or the fact that he was part of her and she knew her own heart.

The vicar was about to speak as he arrived, but the crowd parted to let him through and the vicar hesitated, giving Blake time to be where he needed to be.

By Mardie's side.

Holding Mardie's hand.

The vicar smiled a question—okay to go on?—and he nodded.

It was as if he had the right to be here. As if he had the right to be part of the ceremony for this old dog-trainer, a man who was loved by so many.

Charlie belonged.

As Blake finally belonged.

Mardie's hand tightened on his and he knew it for truth.

It took the rest of the day before he found some time alone with her. The wake was enormous, the pub crowded, and the day turned into an impromptu dog trial.

The football oval was taken over, hurdles, pegs, pens set up. Charlie's dogs versus Charlie's dogs.

Someone thought of a barbecue; parts of the crowd dispersed, came back with supplies. Day turned to dusk turned to dark. The stories of Charlie were legion.

Mardie moved through the crowd with Bessie. It was as if Bessie was part of who Charlie was; it was important that she stayed.

But finally only the diehards were left—old men who'd sit and remember their friend over a beer or six, Charlie's mates.

Mardie was free to leave.

Blake drove her home in her truck. His car was still up on the hill and it was likely to stay there.

There was a thumping sound in the engine. Ominous. He might need to do something about that.

He would. He'd put it on his list. His list for after he'd asked what he needed to ask.

Once again, there was silence in the truck, but it was different. Peace. Acceptance.

The beginning of joy?

He pulled up in the yard. They climbed out, the dogs jumping wearily down after them and heading straight inside, to their basket by the fire. Side by side again.

Joined at the heart.

Like him and this woman by his side.

Mardie let them in and then turned. Blake was right behind her. Close.

Watching her in the moonlight.

'I'm glad you came back,' she said simply.

'I should never have left.'

'You had to leave,' she said softly. 'You know, if you'd told me about Robbie, I would have understood. I understand now how important it was to you. How important it is.'

'It was a process,' he said simply. 'Something I had to work through. Something that started when I was seven, went full circle, then came back to you.'

She stilled, except her heart hadn't stilled. Her heart was hammering as if it might explode.

'You've come back?'

'I love you, Mardie,' he said simple and true. 'Like you... I've loved you all the time without stopping. Things got in the way. I couldn't get perspective. But now...'

'Now?'

'The funeral today,' he said. 'Hundreds of dogs, a funeral procession for one old man. A pilot's wife weeping over a plate. Raff, looking after his community. Harry and Riley at North Coast Rescue. You're all doing what you do, what you love to do, what makes you happy. But you don't destroy yourself in the process.'

'Is that what you've been doing?'

'No,' he said sharply. 'I left here when I was seventeen, and yes, I felt like a martyr then. Heading off to make up for my brother's life. But it changed. It became a passion, a love all on its own. It was only when I couldn't do it any more that shock and illness and a lack of perspective made me go back to the martyr bit.' He reached out and took her hands. 'It took one dog. One dog and one beautiful woman. It took my best friend, Mardie Rainey, to set me right.'

'So...' She was scarcely able to breathe. 'So you're set right now?'

'I have a plan.'

'A plan...'

'It's in its infancy,' he said. 'A bud of a plan. It needs work. It needs an artist to tweak the edges. But you want to hear?'

How could he doubt it? Her face must have answered for her.

'I teach online,' he said simply. 'I'd like to expand that. Medics in remote areas... I'm learning to use Skype so I can talk doctors through procedures. Video links. There's so much. If I stay in the one place, I can be connected all over the world.'

'You'd…be happy with that?'

'No,' he said. 'Not completely. So I will accept Riley and Harry's job offer. Three days a week they do their Outback clinics and they'll fly via here. I can work with them. I can still make a difference. I might,' he added diffidently, 'need to go overseas a couple of times a year, to conferences, to teaching clinics and to keep in touch with the foundation. I can still do fund-raising. And…if you wanted to…you could come with me.'

'Come with you?'

'Not to be taken up with my life,' he said. 'Not to follow my passion. But to follow your own. There'd be things you could do, techniques you could learn. We could learn together. We could…'

He paused. Thought about it.

Dropped to one knee.

'We could marry,' he said.

'Blake…' The whole world held its breath.

'I offered you diamonds,' he said simply. 'In Sydney. It was a stupid, crass thought, nothing more. And you know what? Tonight I don't even have a diamond. I've come unprepared. All I have to offer…' He shrugged. 'No. I don't have anything to offer, Mardie, but I do love you. All I have to offer is my love. I want to share your life. I want to be a part of your life. I love you, I want you, and I want to come home.'

And Mardie stared down at him and felt so much love that she must surely be dreaming.

He was waiting for her to answer. A girl had to think of something.

'So no diamond, huh?' she said cautiously.

'I… No. I can get one, but…'

'And an ancient rust bucket of a car that's still stuck on the hill overlooking Banksia Bay cemetery.'

'I guess…' He sounded confused.

'And the mere possibility—not even confirmed—of a part-time job. Part-time? Haven't you heard the saying? For better or worse but not for lunch.'

'I could...I don't know...take a packed lunch down the paddock every lunchtime. Bounce and I have some learning to do. That could be Bessie's teaching time.'

'So you wouldn't be underfoot?'

'Not very much.'

'But you want to stay here?'

'Wherever you are,' he said simply. 'That's where I want to be, for the rest of my life.' Deep breath. 'Mardie, love, I don't want to hurry you, but this veranda's hard.'

'Is it?' She dropped on her knees before him. 'Oh, yes, so it is. You think we should put some padding on it?'

She sounded hysterical, she thought. She felt hysterical.

He took her hands in his. Hysteria faded.

'No padding,' he said. 'Just a fast answer. Yes or no. Mardie Rainey, I love you with all my heart. I want to be part of your life and I want you to be part of my life, for ever and ever. So there's no ring. I'll buy you one in the future but for now it's just me. Just me, Mardie, nothing else. No shadows. No regrets. Just us. Mardie Rainey, my love, my heart, will you be my wife?'

And she looked into his dear face, the face she'd grown with, the face she'd loved once and loved for ever.

Her Blake.

Her past and her future.

Her best friend.

Hysteria was gone. Doubts were gone—there was nothing but Blake.

'Why, yes, Blake Maddock,' she whispered, 'I believe I will.'

'He's home, too,' Blake said with deep satisfaction.

A simple ceremony on a driveway into a Banksia Bay farm. A driveway lined with ancient gum trees. A man and a woman, husband and wife, with their two dogs pressed together beside them.

The Banksia Bay vicar presiding.

Robbie's ashes had lain in a memorial wall for twenty-five years. Blake had hated them there, so now they'd brought him home, to a place where an ancient gum had once stood, a tree with linked initials, split in the storm.

Robbie's ashes were now scattered in the sunlight, on the earth around a sapling already reaching for the sky.

'No carving,' Blake said sternly to Mardie.

'Not me,' she said virtuously. 'But our children might not be into rules.'

The vicar frowned them down. This was a serious business. He read the blessing and then he smiled.

'This is a good thing to do,' he decreed as he gazed out over the farmland to the sea beyond. He'd heard the simple story and he approved. Now he motioned to the bump Mardie was proudly carrying under her smock. 'The bairn...if it's a boy, will you name him Robbie?'

'She's a girl,' Blake said, hugging his wife close. 'Already confirmed and her name's Oriane. It means dawn.'

'Lovely,' the vicar said, beaming. 'For I don't believe in looking back more than we need. Love continues. As for the rest... The past can get in the way of the future.'

Then he glanced at his watch. 'Speaking of the future, I must go.'

'So must we,' Blake said, smiling and clicking his fingers for the two dogs to join them. 'We have dog trials this afternoon. Today, my wife thinks her dog, Bounce, will beat my dog, Bessie, at the Whale Cove Sheepdog Trials. She's dreaming.'

'He'll do it,' Mardie said. 'If not this month, then next.'

'Only because Bessie needs to retire next month. We're having pups,' he told the vicar. 'Babies all over the place. But, pregnant or not, she'll still beat any dog, hands down. Our Bessie's brilliant.'

'We're all brilliant,' Mardie said. Smiling and smiling. 'Together we can do anything.' She hugged her husband and he hugged her back.

'We can do anything we want,' she said simply. 'Together we're home.'

* * * * *

CLASSIC

Quintessential, modern love stories
that are romance at its finest.

COMING NEXT MONTH
AVAILABLE FEBRUARY 14, 2012

#4291 A BRIDE FOR THE ISLAND PRINCE
By Royal Appointment
Rebecca Winters

#4292 MISS PRIM AND THE BILLIONAIRE
The Falcon Dynasty
Lucy Gordon

#4293 THE COP, THE PUPPY AND ME
Cara Colter

#4294 THEIR MIRACLE TWINS
Baby on Board
Nikki Logan

#4295 DARING TO DATE THE BOSS
Barbara Wallace

#4296 HIS PLAIN-JANE CINDERELLA
In Her Shoes...
Jennie Adams

You can find more information on upcoming Harlequin® titles,
free excerpts and more at www.HarlequinInsideRomance.com.

HRCNM0112

REQUEST YOUR FREE BOOKS!
2 FREE NOVELS PLUS 2 FREE GIFTS!

Harlequin®

From the Heart, For the Heart

YES! Please send me 2 FREE Harlequin® Romance novels and my 2 FREE gifts (gifts are worth about $10). After receiving them, if I don't wish to receive any more books, I can return the shipping statement marked "cancel". If I don't cancel, I will receive 6 brand-new novels every month and be billed just $4.09 per book in the U.S. or $4.49 per book in Canada. That's a savings of at least 14% off the cover price! It's quite a bargain! Shipping and handling is just 50¢ per book in the U.S. and 75¢ per book in Canada.* I understand that accepting the 2 free books and gifts places me under no obligation to buy anything. I can always return a shipment and cancel at any time. Even if I never buy another book, the two free books and gifts are mine to keep forever.

116/316 HDN FESE

Name	(PLEASE PRINT)

Address	Apt. #

City	State/Prov.	Zip/Postal Code

Signature (if under 18, a parent or guardian must sign)

Mail to the **Reader Service:**
IN U.S.A.: P.O. Box 1867, Buffalo, NY 14240-1867
IN CANADA: P.O. Box 609, Fort Erie, Ontario L2A 5X3

Not valid for current subscribers to Harlequin Romance books.

**Are you a subscriber to Harlequin Romance books
and want to receive the larger-print edition?
Call 1-800-873-8635 or visit www.ReaderService.com.**

* Terms and prices subject to change without notice. Prices do not include applicable taxes. Sales tax applicable in N.Y. Canadian residents will be charged applicable taxes. Offer not valid in Quebec. This offer is limited to one order per household. All orders subject to credit approval. Credit or debit balances in a customer's account(s) may be offset by any other outstanding balance owed by or to the customer. Please allow 4 to 6 weeks for delivery. Offer available while quantities last.

Your Privacy—The Reader Service is committed to protecting your privacy. Our Privacy Policy is available online at www.ReaderService.com or upon request from the Reader Service.

We make a portion of our mailing list available to reputable third parties that offer products we believe may interest you. If you prefer that we not exchange your name with third parties, or if you wish to clarify or modify your communication preferences, please visit us at www.ReaderService.com/consumerschoice or write to us at Reader Service Preference Service, P.O. Box 9062, Buffalo, NY 14269. Include your complete name and address.

HRI11B

USA TODAY bestselling author

Sarah Morgan

brings readers another enchanting story

ONCE A FERRARA WIFE...

When Laurel Ferrara is summoned back to Sicily
by her estranged husband, billionaire
Cristiano Ferrara, Laurel knows things are about
to heat up. And Cristiano's power is a potent
reminder of his Sicilian dynasty's unbreakable rule:
once a Ferrara wife, always a Ferrara wife....

Sparks fly this February

*Louisa Morgan loves being around children.
So when she has the opportunity to tutor bedridden Ellie,
she's determined to bring joy back into the motherless
girl's world. Can she also help Ellie's father open his
heart again? Read on for a sneak peek of*

THE COWBOY FATHER

*by Linda Ford,
available February 2012 from Love Inspired Historical.*

Why had Louisa thought she could do this job? A bubble of self-pity whispered she was totally useless, but Louisa ignored it. She wasn't useless. She could help Ellie if the child allowed it.

Emmet walked her out, waiting until they were out of earshot to speak. "I sense you and Ellie are not getting along."

"Ellie has lost her freedom. On top of that, everything is new. Familiar things are gone. Her only defense is to exert what little independence she has left. I believe she will soon tire of it and find there are more enjoyable ways to pass the time."

He looked doubtful. Louisa feared he would tell her not to return. But after several seconds' consideration, he sighed heavily. "You're right about one thing. She's lost everything. She can hardly be blamed for feeling out of sorts."

"She hasn't lost everything, though." Her words were quiet, coming from a place full of certainty that Emmet was more than enough for this child. "She has you."

"She'll always have me. As long as I live." He clenched his fists. "And I fully intend to raise her in such a way that even if something happened to me, she would never feel like I was gone. I'd be in her thoughts and in her actions every day."

Peace filled Louisa. "Exactly what my father did."

Their gazes connected, forged a single thought about fathers and daughters…how each needed the other. How sweet the relationship was.

Louisa tipped her head away first. "I'll see you tomorrow."

Emmet nodded. "Until tomorrow then."

She climbed behind the wheel of their automobile and turned toward home. She admired Emmet's devotion to his child. It reminded her of the love her own father had lavished on Louisa and her sisters. Louisa smiled as fond memories of her father filled her thoughts. Ellie was a fortunate child to know such love.

Louisa understands what both father and daughter are going through. Will her compassion help them heal—and form a new family? Find out in
THE COWBOY FATHER
by Linda Ford, available February 14, 2012.

Discover a touching new trilogy from
USA TODAY bestselling author

Janice Kay Johnson

Between Love and Duty

As the eldest brother of three, Duncan MacLachlan
is used to being in control and maintaining an
emotional distance; as a police captain it's his job.
But when he meets Jane Brooks, Duncan soon finds
his control slipping away. Together, they fight for a
young boy's future, and soon Duncan finds himself
hoping to build a future with Jane.

Available February 2012

From Father to Son
(March 2012)

The Call of Bravery
(April 2012)